DESTINED TO MEET

BY
JOURDYN KELLY

Also by Jourdyn Kelly

Eve Sumptor Novels

Something About Eve
Flawed Perfection
The Truth About Eve
Fighting for Eve

The Destined Series

Destined to Kill
Destined to Love
Destined to Meet

The LA Lovers Series

Coming Home
Fifty Shades of Pink
Coming Out
Becoming
Teach Me (Co-Write with Melissa Tereze)
Coming To
Undoing

CONTENTS

AUTHOR'S NOTE

"CATCHING YOU UP."

D estined to Meet is the third and final book in the Destined Series. To fully understand Anala Geil and her Hunters, I recommend reading Destined to Kill and Destined to Love before diving into Destined to Meet. The Destined Series follows Anala Geil on her journey from Hunter to Cursed Hunter. All Ana wants is to be a normal teenager. The problem is, she's anything but ordinary. Not only is she a Hunter (Cursed Ones beware), she is also Cursed (a vampire) and, well, over 600 years old. Still, she strives to live her life as normally as possible. She has just graduated from high school (again) and has taken her friends—and not-so-friends—along on a trip into her past. It just so happens that those friends are descendants of Hunters, and Ana needs their help.

In this final book, we'll see if Ana, her lover Sam, and her loyal friends/Hunters can face the challenges awaiting them in the land where her life began six centuries ago. One thing Ana knows for certain is that she will do everything in her power to protect those she loves. She's already lost too much, and she isn't sure if her immortal heart can endure any more.

CHAPTER ONE

"WELL PLAYED, TROUBLEMAKER."

"A nala Lagan?"

Amanda's incredulous voice broke through my shocked immobility. Obviously, I heard right if Amanda is saying the same name that is going through my head. Over and over.

"*Impossible.*" My voice is barely above a whisper, and I doubt anyone is even paying attention to me. That is, until I feel Sam's hand resting lightly on my back. Even that gentle touch is enough to ground me.

"Yes." Tania looks confused by my reluctance to believe her. She turns to me, anger flashing in her hazel eyes. "You question my honor?"

"Hold on there, Buffy," Jenna steps between me and Tania, holding her hands up in a placating gesture. I can't help but snicker at her 'Buffy' comment, and she turns to smirk at me before addressing Tania again. "A..., er, *Ella's* not questioning your honor. We just have things we need to discuss. Alone."

Jenna turns and walks confidently out of the room, expecting me to follow her. Damn. This might get complicated. I can't just leave Tania here alone without someone watching her. I haven't known her long enough to trust her.

"Sara?" I beckon. She strides towards me, giving Tania a small smile as she passes.

"You want me to stay and keep an eye on her?" Sara asks quietly.

"Please. We will fill you in on everything when we can. Is that okay?"

I don't want Sara to feel she's not part of the group, no matter how new she is. She has proven herself to me, and even though we have had our disagreements, I trust her to be discreet with Tania. She nods slightly.

"Come." Sara takes Tania by the arm and leads her out towards the kitchen. "Let's see if we can find something suitable to eat. My grandmother could make a delicious meal out of any scraps she found in the kitchen."

I wait until her voice fades away before turning to the others.

"Let's not keep Jenna waiting. No telling what she'll do to us."

"About time. Thought I was going to have to come in there and drag you people out." Jenna pops her gum for good measure, grinning at me when I let out a slight growl.

"How can this be possible?" Sam asks, ignoring Jenna's antics.

"It can't be, as far as I know," I answer. Then again, I had no idea that other Hunters-or 'Enforcers'-were roaming the world, consorting with Cursed Ones. I wonder, if my parents had lived, would I have learned about the others? Why did Papa keep all of this from me? He *must* have known that Cursed Ones and Hunters existed beyond our village. Why keep me in the dark if I were to inherit leadership of the Society? Too many damned questions, and not enough answers.

Perhaps he was trying to protect you.

Sam's voice in my head expressed understanding and compassion, but it didn't help me.

Protecting me involves giving me all the information I need to defend myself.

I briefly touch Sam's arm as a silent apology for my attitude. It still feels strange to me that we can communicate fully without anyone else knowing.

"I need their journals," I say aloud.

"Could Thomas have..." Emily's question was hesitant. I wonder if it's her shyness coming out, or if she's reluctant to speak Thomas's name.

"No. He was turned not long after me."

"But he could have... been with someone before he was turned," Amanda counters.

I pause, contemplating that scenario. Could he have bedded someone else while claiming he wanted to be with me? Hell, at this point, anything is possible. I just don't believe it. I hear Sam's thoughts stir, but he prudently stays quiet. If he feels like I'm hurt by the possibility that Thomas was with someone else, he isn't projecting it. Doesn't matter. Maybe back then, I would have been hurt. But I carry so much hatred for Thomas now after what he did to Sam and Zac that I can't find an ounce of empathy for the boy I knew long, long ago.

"He could have," I concede. "But why call her Anala?"

"Because he was in love with you," Sam answers matter-of-factly.

"We were children, Sam."

"And he allowed himself to be Cursed when he thought something had happened to you. He murdered your parents," he finishes softly.

The pang of guilt and sadness hit me, causing me to tremble.

I'm sorry. I could clearly hear the dismay he felt when Sam made the apology in my mind.

It's true. I respond in kind. *It's fine, baby.*

"Well, we won't know much until we get the journals," I say out loud for everyone to hear.

"We can go tonight." Jeremy cracks his fingers and bounces on his toes as if he's ready for a fight. As proud as it makes me, I can't let them go.

"I'll go," I say. Although my tone indicates I want no arguments, they still argue. What can I tell you? They are my Hunters. I would probably be disappointed if they didn't argue.

"Why should you go alone?" Jenna scoffs.

"Ana, you can't do this alone!" Amanda scolds.

"No way!"

"We'll go with you!"

"What if something happens?!"

Jeremy, Eric, and Emily talk over each other, each raising their voice and becoming more stubborn. The only one I don't hear from—and the one I worry about the most—is Sam. I don't know if I'll get the cooperative Sam or the one who'll be pissed off at me for wanting to handle this alone.

"Look, those guys over there are unpredictable. I will not risk your lives for a few books."

"All the more reason for us to go with you!" Amanda puts her hands on her hips and glares at me. She then turns that glare on Sam. "Will you talk some sense into her! I mean, you're her boyfriend! Maybe she'll listen to you!"

All the others look to Sam expectantly. Clearly, they believe he can change my mind. Maybe if I weren't so cautious about Malcolm's mental state, I would let Sam try. As it stands, after meeting Malcolm, following our flight to England to gather more information about Hunters and Cursed Ones, which we recently learned about, I find myself wondering if his mental well-being is hanging by a thread.

"Will you at least let me go with you?" I hear Sam ask, bringing my attention back to the present.

"You're still new, Sam. I can't take the chance..." I had to curse Sam after Thomas had him beaten to the brink of death. It wasn't something I wanted to do, at least not like that, and not so soon. However, with Amanda begging me, Sam and Amanda's mother asking me for a miracle, and my own desire to keep the man I love with me, I had no other options. I'm still surprised at how well Sam is handling being Cursed. I just can't help being worried that it may change at any moment.

"You don't trust me?

"That's not it!" I pace away, running a hand through my raven hair. I still have the contacts in that I wore to hide my almost transparent eyes, making them closer to their original blue, and they're beginning to irritate me. Sam has contacts as well, to hide the effects of being turned. I stand in front of him and hold his gaze, enjoying the fact that his eyes are close to his golden eyes I adored so much. "I trust you, you must know that. But you have been Cursed for less than two weeks. This is all still new to both of us. Please, Sam. If you go with me, I'll be worried about you, not focused on what I'm supposed to be doing."

Sam's once expressive eyes look dull behind the contacts, but he still nods, acquiescing to my pleas.

"Ugh! Fine!" Amanda throws her hands up in frustration at Sam's seemingly easy surrender. Only I know he's seething inside. "You won't let Sam go, then you're taking at least one of us."

"No."

"Ana!"

"Enough, Amanda! For once, act like I'm your leader and not just your best friend." I soften my voice when I see her flinch at my tone. "I'm not doing this to be difficult. Those people have guns. *Guns*, Amanda. I will not put you in danger like that. How do you think I would feel if you were *killed* because of something I could have easily done myself?"

Amanda opens her mouth, then closes it again, looking genuinely chastised.

"But they're Hunters, Ana," Eric tries reasoning.

"You think I can't handle them?" I raise an eyebrow, put my hands on my hips - much like Amanda - and dare him to say something I don't agree with.

"Of course you can. But we are Hunters. We are your family. You shouldn't *have* to do it on your own. It is *you* who thinks *we* can't handle them."

Well, damn. I challenged him, and he accepted my challenge.

Sigh. "I have faith in all of you and your skills, Eric. But we are not dealing with typical Hunters here. Their guns can kill you without you even knowing they're there. Guns won't hurt me."

Each of them considers my explanation, and I hope they can see my side. Either way, I don't want them putting themselves in danger, but I'd rather they not be upset with me.

"She's right," Jenna finally says. Yeah, I know. I'm just as shocked as you. Jenna and I have recently reached a tentative truce, but I'm still a little surprised when she defends me. "Guns are no joke. As much as I hate for Ana to go by herself, she's the only one—besides Sam—who can do this without getting killed by the stupid freaks."

Ah, there's my Jenna.

Amanda sighs heavily, but she can't argue anymore, which I know is tough for her. Dear, sweet, blond, cheerful Amanda does not like to lose.

"If something happens to you I'll never forgive you," she grumbles, brushing past me to stalk back into the sitting room.

The others glance at me, then at Sam, then back to me. Their excuses for leaving us alone are mumbled quickly and incoherently, and I find myself facing an angry Sam.

"I know you're not happy with me, baby, but . . . "

"Why do you think they couldn't sense me?" he interrupts.

I take a moment to adapt to the course change this discussion just took. I think back to when Sam found out what I really was, and he asked me the same question. 'Why can't I sense you?''

I take a cautious step toward Sam and softly place my palm on his cheek.

"They can't sense you for the same reason you couldn't sense me," I explain softly. "There's not an ounce of evil in you, Sam.

"And, yet, you still think I will lose my humanity at any moment," he murmurs, pulling away. "I guess I don't blame you. Zac's humanity switched off pretty quickly."

"Oh, baby." I summon all my strength to resist going to him and wrapping him in my arms. "Zac already had anger issues. I don't believe he was evil, but I don't think he had a handle on his emotions." I give up trying to stay away from Sam and pray he won't pull away from me again. "I don't think you'll lose your humanity. I really don't know what I'm afraid of. This whole thing seems way too easy," I say.

"I understand that. I saw how Zac was and was worried that it would happen to me. I don't know why I haven't felt the intensity of the effects." He looks almost defeated when he lifts his eyes to mine. "*I'm afraid* . . . "

I pull Sam into my arms and hold him tightly. It's all my fault that he's feeling this fear. If I could stop waiting for the proverbial other shoe to drop, he would be okay. Damn me and my pessimism. Six hundred years of pain and loss can really turn you into a cynic.

"I don't think you have anything to worry about," I confess. "If it hasn't happened yet, I don't believe it will. I've just been overly dramatic and overprotective. I'm sorry."

"So you'll let me go with you?"

I glance up in time to see his charming grin and push him playfully.

"Well played, troublemaker."

"I really was worried. But I'm trusting your judgment. If you're not concerned, I won't be either."

Great. Pressure I don't need.

"I'm not trying to pressure you, baby," he says gently. "Love means trust, right?"

"Right," I grumble. "And, if you go with me, you have to listen to me. You will stay away from the house unless I need you."

"You don't already need me?" he asks seductively.

"Stop it." I tap him lightly on his taut abs. "Of course I need you." I touch my lips to his but pull away before he can deepen the kiss. "Do you agree with my terms?"

"Will you kiss me if I do?"

"Maybe."

"Fine. I will stay in the background. But I *will* be there at the first sign of trouble."

"Deal. Just be sure to keep aware of your surroundings. There's no telling what they do out there."

Sam nods. "Let's talk to Tania. Maybe she can give us a rundown of their setup."

"Good idea. We'll need to find out where Malcolm keeps the journals and get a layout of the house." I start walking toward the sitting room. "Maybe Jenna can find the blueprints on the computer..."

I stop talking abruptly when Sam tugs my arm.

"Where's my kiss? A deal has to be sealed, you know."

I chuckle at his playful smirk.

"Well, far be it from me to not seal a deal." I thread my hands through his wheat-colored hair and bring his lips down to mine. Mmm. This is one hell of a seal.

CHAPTER TWO

"I FAILED ALL OF YOU."

"Thank you for letting Sam go with you."

Amanda pulls me away from the crowd after Tania had given us the information we needed. Jenna is currently looking for blueprints, and the others are milling about talking to Sam about plans. I keep my mind in tune with his even as I turn my attention to Amanda. She looks so different from the girl I met a little more than two years ago. She has the same tawny hair (lightened by sun and product), same golden eyes, but what strikes me the most is the hardness behind those once innocent eyes. The girl who once thought boys, clothes, and parties were the most important things in the world is now a mature young woman. It almost makes me sad that she had to grow up so quickly and see so many terrible things.

"I told you before, Amanda, I'm not trying to be difficult. I'm trying to keep you alive."

"I realize that. I know you're my leader, Ana. I've never forgotten that. But I've never forgotten that we're best friends, either. You can't expect me not to worry about you."

I squeeze her forearm gently.

"I know. How are you doing? We haven't really had a moment to sit down and talk. I should have thought to do that with each of you after..."

I feel the sting of tears as I think of Zac. I can't believe he's gone. It feels like a lifetime ago, yet it was less than two weeks since I killed Zac. *Oh God, I killed Zac.*

"Ana?" I feel Amanda's hand steadying me as I waver.

Sam is beside me in three quick strides.

"Baby?"

"I'm fine." I step back to create space between us.

"What happened?" Concerned eyes plead with her brother to explain what was going on.

"She was thinking about Zac," he relates quietly.

"Tell her the truth, Sam."

"Baby, you had no choice."

"Okay, someone *fill me in*! I mean, *I* can't read your mind, Ana." And there's the hands-on-the-hips-I'm-getting-really-annoyed Amanda I know and love.

"What's going on here?" Jenna walks over carrying what look like printed pages. "Here are the plans for the house."

I take the papers from her, thanking her before turning to Amanda. "I know we don't have a dedicated meditation room here, but could you possibly help us set one up? I can't go into this house," I say, holding up the papers, "feeling like this."

"Of course. Come on, Jenna," Amanda says as she grabs a confused Jenna, dragging her out of the room with her.

I feel guilty about my behavior. My goal was to find out how Amanda was coping with Zac's death, but I got distracted by my own unease. Mom, Dad? Please give me the strength I need to be there for my Hunters. I can immediately feel Sam behind me, wrapping his arms around my waist. With a gentle squeeze, my anxiety begins to fade.

The room is only lit by candlelight, and the gentle aroma of eucalyptus soothes my racing thoughts. There's so much happening, including a 'Priestess' out there bearing my name, that I can't seem to quiet my mind. Of course, it's been like this ever since Bernard found me. I thought that after I killed Thomas, all of this would end. Why does it feel like it's just beginning?

I glance around, amazed by the job Amanda and Jenna did in such a short time. My small Society of Hunters sits on pillows in a circle surrounding a large white candle. The soft flicker of the flame reflects off each of their faces as they silently watch me and wait. Thankfully, Tania had gone to bed, citing a headache. With the way her temples were pulsing, I believed her without a doubt. I'm sorry she's feeling bad, but it works out well for the rest of us because we don't have to censor ourselves around her. So, we set her up in a room on the other side of the house while we gather in our makeshift meditation space.

"Great job," I compliment both Amanda and Jenna, and the others follow suit. "I wanted to meet with you all before we get into all of this 'Priestess' business." I take a deep breath, letting the fragrance in the air envelop me like an invisible cloak of serenity. "The past couple of weeks have been a whirlwind, but I still should have made the time to check in with each of you to see how you were doing. I hope we can get whatever we need out in the open. And while it will be a long time before we begin to feel even a little bit back to normal, hopefully we will be able to give our full concentration to whatever lies ahead."

I pause, waiting for someone to speak up. But everyone drops their gaze when I look at them.

"Okay," I sigh. "I'll begin."

I pause for a moment to try and find the words for my feelings. How can I tell them how much I ache for what I had to do to Zac? How do I explain the guilt?

Open your heart, baby. They will understand. Trust them to support you just as much as you want to support them.

My eyes track to Sam, and I allow the intense love I feel for him to shine through.

"First, I want to apologize to all of you." I hold my hand up when I see them begin to argue. "Please, let me finish. I am your leader. It is natural for me to feel responsible for each of you. Zac was turned on my watch. I couldn't save him." I pause again, warring with myself about how much to tell them. And I know, without a doubt, they should know everything. "He told me he didn't want to live...this way, but I believed that I, that *all* of us could help him make the transition. His deteriorating condition should have warned me to be more diligent with his care. I could sit here and try to analyze every single thing that I did, that he said, that we saw, but it all ends the same way. Zac is dead by my hand. He was our friend, our family, our fellow Hunter, and I failed him. I failed all of you. I failed Sam." My voice wavers at this point, but I continue before anyone can say anything. "I swear to you, I will do everything in my power to keep all of you alive. You all deserve that and more for what you have sacrificed for me."

A tear slides down my cheek before I can stop it, but I don't care. I want them to see that I hurt just as much as they do. This isn't the time to hide my feelings from them.

"Ana." Amanda's soft voice carries through the quiet room. The compassion and understanding I hear in just the way she says my name is almost my undoing. "I feel like I speak for us all when I say none of this is your fault." She looks around, making sure she has everyone's agreement before continuing. "I know that I was one of the worst when it came to blaming you, and I can't begin to apologize enough for that."

When Sam was in the hospital, dying, Amanda's emotions overwhelmed her when I refused to do what she asked and turn Sam. She blamed me for what had happened. And that, along with Sam's condition, my killing Thomas, the burden of Zac's situation, my parents' deaths, and a long, lonely life, caused my humanity to falter.

"You are the one who brought me back," I remind her.

"I'm the one who put you in that position in the first place. Wait," she holds up a finger, effectively cutting off my rebuttal. "I *knew* you already felt guilty. I used that against you. I was so pissed off and scared that I would do anything to change your mind about Sam. What I did was wrong. They all let me know that," she says, jerking her thumb towards the others. "They helped me see the error of what I did. And as much as I hate what happened to Zac, I trust you implicitly. He was too far gone for us to save. *Us*, Ana. You may have held the sword, but we stood beside you. Yes, it hurts. I feel his loss every day. But our reality... if we don't move on with our lives by putting the past behind us, we will end up the same way."

Amanda leans forward, placing her hand on top of mine.

"Your actions are made to keep us and other innocents safe. How can we possibly fault you for that?"

Sam places his hand over Amanda's, and I watch in stunned silence as Jenna, Jeremy, Sara, Eric, and even Emily join in, putting their hands in as a sign of solidarity with me and our Society. A complete and utter calm washes over me—something I haven't felt since Bernard reappeared in my life.

We face a huge challenge ahead, but because our bond has been strengthened, I believe we will overcome whatever difficulties come our way.

CHAPTER THREE

"WE'RE NOT ALONE."

Sam and I enter the woods, taking the trail Tania told us about. If we can trust her, the trail should lead right to the Enforcers'...home? Hideout? Whatever it is to them, I want to get there undetected. I don't know Tania, so my trust in her only goes so far. My senses kick in on their own - a side effect of being worried about my surroundings - and I stop so abruptly that Sam has no choice but to run into me.

"Sorry," he murmurs before I have a chance to stop him from speaking.

Quiet. We're not alone.

Closing my eyes, I focus intently on my heightened abilities, trying to determine what we're up against.

I sense them. They're not...human.

No, they're not, I silently agree with Sam. They're cursed. Whether the Cursed Ones are working for the Enforcers, I don't know. What I do know is that I don't sense humans. I'm not sure whether to be grateful for that or pissed off. On one hand, no humans means no guns. On the other hand, Hunters should be patrolling and keeping their area safe. Sigh. I really need to find out what's going on around here.

How many are there?

I close my eyes, picking out the differences in each scent. One thing I know for sure is they are all full bloods. Five distinct scents. I hold up five fingers to Sam and watch him nod.

We can handle that.

His confidence makes me smile. While I am sure we can handle it, I don't want to draw unnecessary attention in case there are Hunters - excuse me, 'Enforcers' - in the area that I just don't sense. As soon as those thoughts enter my mind, my nose picks up six more extremely familiar scents. Damn it! I tug Sam back toward where we entered the woods, approaching my Hunters.

"What are you doing here? I thought I made it clear that Sam and I would be doing this alone." My tone, I'm sure, makes it clear that I am not a happy leader.

"We had a feeling you could use our help," Amanda bravely answers. Her shoulders are squared, and her head is held high as if she's daring me to argue. It takes an extraordinary amount of restraint not to laugh at their independence. Even if they were directly disobeying me. I focus on making my glare menacing. And though I don't mean it, it makes my Hunters take a step back.

"Lucky for you, there are Cursed Ones here, and no humans that I can tell." I allow a small smile to replace my scowl. "But you cannot go any farther than these woods. I will handle everything else. That is not open for debate. Is that clear?"

Jenna steps forward, her hand lightly resting on her sword. "Tania mentioned something about Malcolm having Cursed Ones roaming the woods to keep away unwanted guests. She thought we should warn you."

"Why didn't she mention that before?" I wonder aloud.

"Good question. I don't trust her," Emily complains. "There are too many holes in her story."

"Do you think she's setting us up?" I ask the group, anxious to hear their opinions.

"I think she wants you to kill Malcolm," Jeremy answers, and I can't help but be impressed with his intuition. I had thought the same thing, but just because she wants something doesn't mean it'll happen.

"You may be right. She saw what I did to Meathead," I begin, thinking of Meathead (aka Gunner, the enormously muscular 'right-hand man' of Malcolm's). The last time we met, Gunner delivered a message from Malcolm to me. In other words, he punched me in the face. I know! What kind of 'gentleman' punches a girl? I had no other choice but to return the message. As far as I know, Gunner went back to Malcolm with a broken jaw and broken nose. "I'm sure she thinks anyone who can handle steroid-man can rid her of her problematic brother."

"Are you planning to kill him?"

My eyebrows shoot straight up to my hairline at Amanda's question. I honestly thought she knew me better than that. I don't kill innocents.

"I mean, I totally would after what I've seen of him, and what he had his buffoon do to you," she hurriedly explains.

"No, you wouldn't. He's an innocent. And possibly a fellow Hunter. We can't kill him," I say dryly, and see her shoulders droop at my reprimand. "That doesn't mean I'm not going to make sure he got my message loud and clear if he interferes with my objective."

I smile at their chuckles, thinking about how great it is that we've become so close during our time together. I guess what they say about what doesn't kill you makes you stronger applies to us as a group.

"Alright, enough standing around. I'll let you handle this mess in the woods. Be extra careful, though, they're Full Bloods. I'm not sure how old they are, so they might pose a problem for you. I'll stay with you just long enough to make sure..."

"We know what we're doing, Ana."

My eyes cut to Jenna.

"I abhor being interrupted, Jenna, especially when I am trying to explain my intentions."

"Sorry."

As I was saying, I'll stay with you long enough to make sure they don't have guns or anything else that could hurt you. I also want to see what we're up against with these Full Bloods to figure out their ages. If they're from my time, you might have a hard time. Not," I say quickly at my Hunters' narrowed eyes, "because I don't think you can handle them. You've handled me just fine. But I'm only one.

There are five of them out there. We don't know how trained they are or if, like Thomas's group, they are swordsmen. Does that satisfy you, Jenna?"

She shrugs but offers me a small smile.

"Good. Be alert. Hold nothing back. Ready?"

My Hunters draw their swords, pressing buttons to release the blades. I nod to them, lifting the hood of my cloak. If we lose one of them somehow, I can't have them returning to Malcolm with my description, especially since I'm pretty sure they're about to find out I'm one of them.

We move into the woods quietly, spreading out enough to cover ground but staying close enough to watch each other's backs. They look to me for directions, and I use hand signals to show where the Cursed Ones are. The closest one is a little over a football field away. They're scattered and staggered as they wander through the woods. That's good for us because they won't gang up on us—at least not before we reach our first target.

They might be able to sense you as you approach. I tell Sam silently. Cursed Ones usually detect the presence and smell of another Cursed One; however, none have managed to detect me. I can't help but wonder if Sam will be the same way. Sam nods but stays aligned with me. *Let them handle it. Only step in if necessary.* I feel Sam's hand brush my lower back, and a jolt of electricity runs through me from the simple touch. *Oh boy.* It'll be nice when we finally get a chance to just get to know each other without anything else going on. When Sam chuckles softly, I know he agrees wholeheartedly.

I tap Amanda lightly on the shoulder and point to her left. She quickly takes her position while I silently give orders to the others. We're effectively closing in on the first Cursed One, and I confirm that the others are still some distance away. I leave it up to them how to handle the situation. I'm just here to observe. At least, I hope so.

Jeremy takes point with Emily and Eric flanking him. They are perfectly in sync, needing no words to communicate. I pause to feel proud before being truly impressed by their plan.

As Jeremy, Emily, and Eric approach the Full Blood, Jenna, Amanda, and Sara move soundlessly out of sight, but never so far that they can't be there immediately if needed. To my surprise, the first three hide their swords and advance amiably. Just a stroll in the woods.

"Excuse me? We must be turned around. Do you know how to get back to the road?"

It's so unbelievable to me that I almost laugh out loud. My Hunters know that Cursed Ones can tell if someone is a Hunter. However, if these Cursed Ones are working with the Enforcers, they might be respectful. Very smart, I think as more pride flows through me.

"Who are you?" the Cursed One snarls. There's no doubt this guy is Cursed with that voice. He's not big at all, at least two inches shorter than Sam's six foot four frame, and he's not very well defined. Gangly would be the first word that comes to mind. But I know looks don't tell the whole story. This Full Blood will be quick and nimble as well as strong. Being this close, I can sense more about the Full Blood, and the smell of his blood is old, though I don't think he's as old as me. Just that knowledge relaxes me a bit.

"We're just hikers, man. No biggie. Just a little turned around."

"Are you Malcolm's?"

The question makes me bristle. No, damn it, they're not Malcolm's! Sam's hand tightens around my bicep, stopping me as I inch forward.

"Trying to be, man. You know how it is. They won't take her, though." Jeremy jerks his thumb at Emily. Good strategy, Jeremy!

The Cursed One actually smiles as if he understands. "She'll make a good servant," he rasps.

Ohh, I can see Emily stiffen from my vantage point. I don't blame her. I also notice that Jeremy and Eric take a step back as the other girls step forward next to Emily. Huh. Interesting. They're about to show this Full Blood just what girls can do.

"Servant my ass," Emily retorts and punches him in the face, stunning him for a fraction of a second. But no matter how quick he is, my Hunters are ready. The girls side-step his advance, and Emily, with help from Jenna, donkey kicks him in the back, making him stumble and fall forward. Not surprisingly, the guys stay back, knowing the girls will have no problems.

The Full Blood growls and scrambles up. As much as I want my girls to show this ass who's boss, I'm hoping they hurry and not play with him for too long. We have things to do, and we don't need the other Full Bloods showing up to investigate. As if they read my mind, each of them has their swords ready for when the Full Blood charges again. Amanda rams her sword through his chest, rendering him useless. By some silent agreement, Emily makes the kill shot by bringing her sword down across his neck.

"Teach you to call me a servant," Emily mumbles before turning to me. "What can you tell about him?"

Besides his being as big an ass as Malcolm?" I ask, making her smile. "He's old, but not as old as I am. Not a word, Jenna!" I give a mock glare at Jenna. I just know she wants to make a smart-ass remark about my age, but she actually stays quiet. "I'm impressed with all of you. Jeremy, that approach was genius."

Jeremy's chest puffs out with pride before he confesses that they had talked about their strategy beforehand.

"Did you notice that he seemed a bit scared of Malcolm?" Eric asks the group. "His eyes darted as if he were expecting Malcolm to suddenly pop out."

The others nod their agreement. The observation doesn't make me happy. If the Full Blood was expecting an appearance, that means Malcolm or Meathead could show up at any time.

"Take care of the others and do it quickly. Then I want all of you out of here." Sam's eyes whip to me.

"Except for you, Sam. I've already agreed to that. Just remember what you agreed to. You can make sure everything goes according to plan out here, then follow me to the edge of the woods. I'm trusting you to stay back, Sam."

"I will stay back unless I feel you need help. That's my deal, Anala. I will not leave you behind."

CHAPTER FOUR
"LUCKY."

One thing I can say I completely adore about being Cursed is my ability to almost fly. Okay, so I'm not really flying; I'm more like a spider monkey. I can use the trees to move closer to the house without being noticed. The leaves make no sound as I leap from branch to branch. I take advantage of my vantage point, making sure my Hunters are doing well and gauging the distance to the house. There's a large chasm between the woods and the house. It looks like my 'flying' ability is about to be put to the ultimate test.

I evaluate the strength of the branch I'm on, hoping it's sturdy enough to handle the force I'll exert. Some of the English Oaks in this forest are hundreds of years old - yes, even older than me - and are healthily durable. I'm fairly confident that my platform will be more than sufficient for my needs.

Be careful, baby.

Sam's voice in my head startles me enough to almost make me lose my footing.

Sam!

I can actually feel his humor as I hear his snickers in my head.

Sorry.

I smile at his completely unrepentant apology and assure him that I'll be just fine. Hell, even if I don't reach the house, I'll still land on my feet. It's not like a fall will hurt me. As soon as that thought leaves my mind, I notice a glint of something in the lawn ahead. I squint to focus all my heightened vision on that tiny shimmer.

"What in the hell is that?" I whisper to, well, no one since I'm alone.

Baby?

I feel Sam getting closer to me...to the edge of the forest.

Wait, Sam! Don't move!

I silently drop down beside Sam. I wrap my hand around his bicep, pulling him back a step. I point toward the glint.

"Do you see that?"

Sam follows my finger, squinting too. I understand he's still adjusting to his new abilities, and it takes him a bit more time to focus.

"What is it?"

"I believe the area is booby trapped," I explain, now noticing more gleams surrounding the house.

"Are you shitting me?" Jenna exclaims, startling me once again because I'm so fixated on what's in front of me.

"Hush!" I glare at her, not just for her practically yelling during a stealth operation, but for being here. "I thought I told you guys to finish up and leave!" I hiss through gritted teeth.

"We just finished, Ana. We heard you talking about booby traps, so we came over," Amanda explains casually.

"This is just one more thing Tania didn't tell us," Emily grumbles. "Something is really wrong here."

"Maybe she didn't know about it," Sara says, playing Devil's advocate. Snorts of disbelief are heard from more than one of her fellow Hunters.

"Sara is right," I say before any arguments can start. I have to remember that no matter how much these kids have gone through in the past few weeks, they are still kids. Emotions and hormones are going to clash from time to time. They're still learning to control those emotions. "From what I have noticed, Malcolm does not share his plans with anyone of the female persuasion. Tania was a mere servant to him."

"But she's his sister," Jenna argues.

"And you saw how he treated her," I counter. "No acknowledgement. He dismissed her just as quickly as he did the rest of us. There is no love lost between them. I'm still with Eric. I think she wants me to kill Malcolm. I don't think she knows about the traps."

The others reluctantly accept my explanation, choosing to hold off judgment until they have more details. That's all I can reasonably ask of them. As for me, I don't trust Tania at all, but I'm prepared to follow through on what I ask of my Hunters until I find out everything I need to know. My first challenge is figuring out how to reach the house without getting impaled by whatever's hidden in the ground. I really do think I can make the leap...

"What if you miss?" Sam asks softly.

"Then I try to angle myself away from anything that's shiny," I answer glibly, much to Sam's disappointment.

"Okay, we obviously don't know what's going on. Which one of you wants to explain the plan?" Jenna asks haughtily.

"The *plan* is that *you* are going back to the house. *I* am going to find my way over there," I point to Malcolm's glum dwelling, "and get the journals."

"And how do you propose to get over there, seeing that the entire yard seems to be prepared to kill you with one wrong step?" Amanda's hands are on her hips again, and the look in her eyes makes me think she is *not* happy with my plan at all.

"I'm going to jump from up there," I answer, gesturing to the branches above me.

Here goes nothing.

Much to my dismay, my Hunters disobey me - again - by staying behind. They said it was so they could help if I 'didn't make it.' But I think they just want to watch my attempt. We really need to have a discussion about who the leader is and what that leader expects. Anyway, back to my task at hand. I have to clear my mind and focus.

"Dang Hunters are going to be the death of me," I mutter, causing Sam to chuckle. Yes, I see the damned irony.

Standing on the thickest branch of the nearest tree, I take a deep breath and bend my knees to lower my center of gravity. I focus on the small flat roof covering a balcony, hoping to everything that's holy that it won't cave in beneath me *if* I land on it.

I push off the branch with my powerful legs, and I hear it crack and fall behind me with a forceful sound. I lengthen my body to make it more aerodynamic as my cloak streams behind me. I know I'm holding my breath, trying to stay positive as I pass the halfway point. Damn it, it feels like I'm flying in slow motion! In reality, I hit the roof within seconds of my takeoff, and my feet immediately slide over the shingles. I use my hands, trying to grab anything I can to stop myself from going over the edge.

Shit! I feel my feet slip off the edge of the balcony, and I can actually hear the gasps from my Hunters still in the woods. At least they better still be in the woods, I think as my hands grip the edge of the roof. I take a moment to breathe and take in my surroundings as I dangle by my fingertips. Too damned close.

I drop softly onto the balcony and peek through the double doors into what looks like a study. Lucky. The journals should be in this room, hidden behind a trap statue. That's if Tania was telling me the truth. Hopefully, my luck holds, and the damned room isn't booby-trapped like the yard is.

Make them leave. I tell Sam. I do not want them to be around if something goes wrong here.

They're going, baby. Be careful. I'm going to look around and see if I can find another way over there.

No! Stay there. Please?

Anala, you're going to have to trust that I know what I'm doing. I may be newly Cursed, but I've been a cop for years.

Sigh. I know he's right, and I really don't want to be standing here arguing with Sam while I'm trying to break into an Enforcer's house.

Fine. But I swear, if you get hurt, I will not forgive you.

I feel the vibration of his soft laughter rumble through me, making me shiver. An entire lifetime of this feeling I have with Sam. That's what I want. Don't take that away from me, I think, knowing Sam would hear me.

I place my hand on the lever-style doorknob, noticing it's locked. With a quick tug, I pull the door open. I brace myself, expecting to hear some kind of alarm or maybe have poison darts shoot at my face. I laugh at the silliness of that image. Maybe I should have worn a fedora and carried a whip instead of my cloak hood and swords. I feel like Indiana Jones dealing with these idiotic traps in the yard. Now, let's see what I'm facing inside.

Gingerly, I step over the threshold. No trip wires so far. Perhaps the Idiot Society is afraid of darting their own faces if they rig up the inside. Ooh, I wonder if anyone forgot that the yard is full of shiny, sharp things and went out there to take a leak. Heh.

You're very entertaining, baby.

Oh lord. I forgot I have company in my brain.

Sam.

I know, I know. But it's not like we've had time to work on me staying out of your thoughts. Besides, I'm making sure you're okay. Obviously you are.

Can you get near the house?

Yes, if I walk up to the front door. They're actually smart enough not to trap a way in and out of the house. But I'm staying back for now. And, before you ask, I'm very aware of my surroundings.

I know you are. I'm going to get those journals, then I'll be out.

How will you get back to the woods?

I'm going to go out the front door.

Chapter Five

"NOOKIE"

The ridiculousness of these 'Enforcers' is almost laughable. And I say almost because I really just want to kick their asses for the theatrics. Seriously? The booby traps, the gothic house, the hidden journals. If I wasn't standing here in this hideous house, surrounded by overgrown idiots and the dramatic measures they're taking to seem important, I wouldn't believe it. I can smell them. They're either sleeping or passed out because I smell the strong odor of alcohol all around.

I move closer to the statue that Tania mentioned, staring at it. A gargoyle? Jesus, this really feels like a role-playing game to these weirdos. They're going to regret getting involved with all of this now that I'm here.

Tentatively, I touch the statue, moving it slightly to one side. When it doesn't budge, I try twisting it. It makes a faint hissing sound, like the inside is air-pressurized. I look around before reaching inside. There's a stack of about seven books that I can see. It can't possibly be all of them if they're supposed to be as old as I am. Even though they're thick, six centuries' worth of information would surely fill more than seven books.

I shrug, hoping that since these are hidden, they are the ones that are the most important. I extract the top book and begin flipping through it quickly, stopping when I notice something is off with these journals. Running my fingers over the pages, I immediately recognize what's wrong. These journals are not the originals. Mere copies. Makes sense, I suppose. I never thought to consider what made Malcolm important enough to the Priestess to have the originals. Obviously he's not. Now the question is, does the Priestess give all of her 'Rulers' copies, or did Malcolm get these by some other means?

"So many damned questions and not enough answers," I mumble to the empty room.

Baby, a light just came on. South side. If I remember correctly, that's the kitchen.

Got it. Keep an eye on it. I have the journals. Once the light goes off, let me know. I'd like to get out of here. Gives me the creeps.

I throw the books into the messenger bag I have strapped around me under my cloak and put the statue back in place.

"Ugly ass thing." I want to smash the damn thing, but I don't think that's a good idea since I'm trying to stay undercover.

Sam?

Light is off, baby. Everything looks quiet.

Okay. I'm going to make a run for it. Meet me in the woods.

I crack open the door to the hallway, using my heightened senses to ensure I won't have any company on my way to the front door. Once I'm sure I'm alone, I quietly close the door behind me and use my speed to reach the end of the hallway in less than a second. Next obstacle, the stairs. I obviously can't see around the corners, so I rely on my other senses to guide me. I briefly close my eyes to picture the layout of the house in my head. Right, and I'm in the living room. Left, the kitchen. So, I'll go straight. Even if the door is locked, it won't stop me.

Taking a deep breath, I secure the messenger bag and dash for the door. I grab the handle and immediately feel my strength waning. Silver. Luckily, drinking from Sam makes silver less effective on me. I still don't know why, but I'm not complaining. I consider just yanking the door open, but that would break the deadbolt and door jam. Instead, I take my time to unlock the door and slip out.

"Hey."

Sam stands there with a wicked grin, and I know exactly what he's thinking. Again, I'm glad I can't blush.

"Hey, yourself," he smirks. "I never realized how entertaining it is to be in your head."

"Ha. Ha." I gently backhand his abs, secretly loving how hard they are. I see his grin widen, and I realize it's not so secret. Sigh. "Let's go before we get unwanted company."

Sure. Just tell me we'll be able to get a little time to ourselves. Please?" Sam suddenly becomes serious. Our bond grows every day, and it has been hard to find alone time to explore that connection. Not to mention that our hunger for each other—in many ways—is increasing. I, for one, will be glad when all of this is over and we can start our eternity together.

"We'll make time, baby. I promise."

I unceremoniously throw the messenger bag full of books onto the dining room table. The others jump at the loud thump, but honestly, I'm too irritable to care. The trek back from the Enforcers' place was tense, to say the least. Sam was especially quiet. Even in his head, which I found disconcerting. His hands, however, were not as quiet. He couldn't keep from touching me—holding my hand, touching my thigh, pushing my hair behind my ear, brushing my cheek with the back of his fingers. And I felt each one of those touches in my (hopefully existing) soul.

By the time we arrived back at our rented house, I couldn't concentrate on anything besides being alone with Sam. This *thing* that's between us is stronger than anything I've ever felt before. And I don't believe that it's just because I'm his Maker. That's merely intensifying the feelings. I was destined to be a killer. It was why I was born. I never, even with Thomas, believed that love was in my future. But now, with Sam? I can't imagine living without it any longer. I can't help but think that Sam and I were destined to meet.

"I would like for you all to start reviewing these journals. They're not the originals, so I'm unsure if anything has been altered. Just make notes about what you think is important for us to know. And if there are questions, we'll ask Tania about it." I turn my attention to Amanda. "Could I see you for a minute?"

Amanda nods, and if the others had a problem with my singling her out, they don't show it. Instead, they each grab a book and start reading. I'm utterly surprised. Had Hell frozen over? I gave an order, and there were no arguments, no sighs, no rolling of the eyes? Unbelievable.

"What's up?" Amanda glances over her shoulder, focusing on the journals. If recent history is any indication, she can't wait to dive into those books. She was practically obsessed with the journals I wrote, needing to carefully analyze every word, sacrificing sleep, eating, and even talking. You know it's serious when Amanda stops talking.

"Are you guys going to be okay going over this by yourself for a while?" I ask quietly.

"Sure. I mean, it's only been about a week since we've graduated, but I'm sure we still know how to read."

Her sarcasm makes me want to smile, but I give her a mock glare instead.

"Funny, funny girl," I mutter.

Amanda glances at Sam, who is waiting patiently - or maybe not so patiently, since he's shifting from one foot to the other. She leans in closer, lowering her voice. "Is something wrong?"

I wonder if she realizes that no matter how low her voice is, Sam can hear her.

"We need some time. Alone."

Amanda just stares at me for a minute.

"You're leaving us to do this because you want some *nookie*?" she asks incredulously.

Great. The time I *want* her to be quiet, and she nearly shouts my very private intentions.

"*Will you keep it down*!" I whisper fiercely. Of course, the damage is already done, as I hear Jenna snicker, and a glance shows me the sly grins from the boys and blushes from the other girls. I grab Amanda's arm and lead her further away. "It's not like that. I can't explain this to you. At least not right at this moment, but it's not about...*nookie*!"

Amanda must have noticed what I assume is an almost desperate look on my face. She gives me a quick hug, then nudges me toward Sam.

"We'll be here. Take all the time you need."

Sam lightly touches my arm as I walk past him into our bedroom. I turn to face him, wrapping my arms around his neck.

"Ever since you turned me," he began, burying his face in my neck, "I haven't experienced the overwhelming hunger. At least not in the way I thought I would."

"What do you mean?"

"My hunger...is for you. Your scent, your blood. Your body." His arms tighten around my waist, pressing me to him. "Your love," he murmurs.

"I've felt the same," I confess. The only way I can explain this is that I was in love with Sam when I turned him. It's the only thing that makes sense.

"I love you, Anala."

"I love you, too, Sam."

"When all of this is over, we need to have a serious discussion about the future."

His mischievous grin makes me chuckle. The kiss he gives me on my neck effectively stops that chuckle, turning it into a groan. When I feel his teeth graze me, I lose all coherent thought completely.

CHAPTER SIX

"HANDS OFF."

"**W**ould you like a sandwich or something?" I carefully maneuver the milk and water bottles in front of the bottles of blood in the refrigerator, then turn to a surprised Tania.

"How did you?"

"I heard you," I interrupt. "Are you hungry?"

"Not really. I just came in for a water and possibly some aspirin."

I look closely at Tania and see the veins throbbing in her temple. I also notice the sweat beading on her forehead. I reach into the refrigerator and take out a bottle of water.

"What did he have you on?" I ask as I hand her the bottle. I don't know why I am so convinced that Malcolm has something to do with Tania's condition, but the feeling is strong.

"Excuse me?"

"You're shaking and sweating. Your head is pounding. You're going through withdrawals. What did he have you on?"

"I don't know what you're talking about."

I study her, seeing only truth and confusion in her eyes. She really has no idea that Malcolm has been drugging her, and I don't think she was willingly doing drugs. I wonder if that's how he keeps all of his Enforcers in line.

31

"Sit." I guide Tania to a chair, feeling the clamminess of her skin. "This is going to get much worse for you before it gets better. Have you been feeling nauseous?"

Tania nods her head weakly. I can almost hear the pounding in her head, and I can't help but feel sorry for her.

"I thought I was having a migraine," she confides. "You really think my brother has been drugging me?"

"The symptoms are there," I shrug. I'm not 100% sure, of course, but close. "There's not much I can do for you except make sure you stay hydrated. Water will be the best thing for you for now. I'm afraid you won't be able to keep any food down, but would you like to try to eat something light?"

She shakes her head and puts a hand over her stomach. "I don't think that's a good idea." Suddenly, Tania looks up at me with an unreadable look. "Did you get what you needed?"

"Yes. We were able to get the journals."

"Is Malcolm dead?"

Well. Eric was right. This is *not* something I want to deal with. Don't I have enough?

"No," I answer forcibly. "I was able to get in and out without being detected."

Tania's face registers complete shock. It makes me wonder if she has asked others to get the books for her before, with poor results.

"How?"

Tania can't finish her question before she doubles over in pain. I'm conflicted. I'm angry that she used me to try to get rid of her brother, even though I understand her desire to be free of Malcolm. But I also don't want to see her suffer. Realizing there's nothing I can do for her, I set the garbage can in front of her - just in case - and gently rub her back for comfort.

"Try to breathe through the pain. When you can sit up again, drink as much of the water as you can."

"An . . . "

Amanda stops abruptly when she sees Tania. I struggle to remember that I am 'Ella' to Tania, so I can only imagine how difficult it is for my Hunters to adjust. I wish I had just stuck with Ana.

"What's going on?"

I glance up at Amanda just as Tania starts retching. Oh lord. Not only do I *hate* getting sick myself, but I also really don't have the stomach for seeing others either. But I force myself to stay next to Tania, holding her blonde locks back.

"Withdrawals," I explain while trying to keep from joining Tania.

Amanda turns around, clearly not wanting to watch what's happening. I don't blame her at all.

"I don't understand."

"I believe Malcolm has been drugging Tania. I don't know if he's doing the same to the others. For now, we just need to help Tania get through this.

"What can I do?" Amanda rests her head on the wall near the entrance. "*Ugh, so gross,*" she mutters. I'm sure she didn't mean for anyone to hear, but... well, you know my hearing. I struggle not to laugh since the situation is so not funny at all.

"Not much we can do except let her ride it out. Can you get another bottle of water? She's going to need it."

Amanda gave us a wide berth, taking the long way around to the refrigerator. I'm pretty sure she's just as grateful as I am when Tania finally stops dumping her guts in the trash can.

"What else?" she asks, as she sets the bottle down next to me.

"Let's get her back to her room. She's going to start shaking soon. I want to make her as comfortable as possible."

"Baby?" Sam walks into the kitchen while Amanda and I help Tania stand. I could easily pick her up and carry her to her room, but obviously that wouldn't be the best choice. "I thought you were coming right back, so I figured I'd come look for you. Everything okay?"

"Sorry. Tania needs a little help. We were just about to take her upstairs."

Sam strides over to us, his eyes narrowing as he studies Tania's face. "She's going through withdrawals?"

I nod, slipping my arm around Tania to hold her up.

"Here, let me." Sam gently nudges Amanda aside and takes Tania from me. He lifts her up, cradling her against his chest like a baby.

I try to hold back my jealousy. I honestly do. But seeing Tania in Sam's arms, and watching her look up at him with obvious attraction, makes my blood boil.

I feel nothing for her, baby. You're the only one for me. Sam clearly feels my simmering rage.

Just get her upstairs quickly. I don't think she feels the same way you do.

Sam gives me a quick nod and heads toward Tania's room with Amanda and me in tow.

"Are you okay? You're extremely tense," Amanda whispers close to my ear.

"Fine."

Amanda places a tentative hand on my arm, and she must have felt my muscles coil like a snake because she jerks her hand back quickly.

"You know he would never . . . "

"I know!" I don't mean to be so harsh with Amanda, but I just watched Tania's hand creep into Sam's hair. She'd better watch it. Sick or not, I'm about to kick her ass.

We're almost there, baby. I'm not enjoying this any more than you.

Sam's words in my head calm me a little. Only a little. But if she keeps twirling her fingers in Sam's hair . . .

I push the door to Tania's bedroom open - perhaps a little too forcefully - urging Sam to hurry and deposit her on the bed. When she holds on a little longer than is respectable, I can't help but step in.

"Hands off," I growl. "I'm trying to help you, Tania, but if you keep touching my boyfriend like that, I will throw you out the window and let you fend for yourself. Or I'll take you back to your brother."

Tania yanks her hands away from Sam and shrinks back into her pillows. She looks as if she might either get sick again or cry. Frankly, I don't give a damn if she does either.

Sam starts to speak, but the look on my face makes him hesitate. He simply walks over to me, kisses my cheek, says he'll see me later in our room, and then leaves. Amanda, however, has no problem smirking at me with a wink.

"I'm sorry." Tania sounds genuinely contrite, though I'm not sure I believe she's truly sorry. The apology doesn't quite reach her eyes. There's just something off about the real 'Ruler' of this territory.

The solid smack of my fist against the plastic of the fighting dummy in the exercise room does nothing to quiet my rage. How dare she touch Sam that way? He's *mine*! *SWACK!* I bring her in, help her, and she repays me by showing interest in what's mine?! I land a perfect roundhouse kick to the dummy, snapping it off its pedestal and sending it across the room.

"Who pissed in your bottle of blood?"

I whirl around, striking out at Jenna. I'm especially glad that she has extraordinary reflexes.

"What the hell!"

"Jesus! Jenna, I am so sorry!" I sink to my knees, trying to clear my mind of Tania.

"What's going on with you?"

I sigh deeply, gathering my hair in my hands to tie it back in a ponytail. "Tania," I answer as if that explains everything.

"What did Buffy do now?"

I can't help but laugh. Call me crazy, but I really am beginning to like Jenna a lot.

"She's going through withdrawals," I begin, and explain everything that's going on. "*Buffy* couldn't keep her damned hands off of Sam."

"Wow. Chick must have a death wish."

"You think?"

"So, that's why you're down here instead of up with your stud muffin?"

"I just needed to blow off some steam."

"Can't you do that with Sam?" Jenna smirks.

"Ha." I lie back with my hands behind my head, my knees bent, and tap my toes. "I was afraid of what I might have done in my state." It was true. I've never felt jealousy at this level. Hell, I've never experienced jealousy at all. It wasn't an emotion that was needed in my life. I had always thought it was a foolish emotion. Or perhaps I have just never felt the depth of emotion I feel for Sam. What I know now is I hate this feeling, and it leaves me with enough fear of my own rage to stay away from the one I love the most.

"I'm sure Sam thanks you then," she teases. "Did you see Amanda yet?"

"I saw her earlier. Why?"

"Did she tell you anything about the journals?"

I sit up abruptly. "No, I haven't given her a chance. What did you find?"

One good thing about being a vampire is that I don't need sleep. On the other hand, one bad thing about being a vampire is that I don't need sleep. So, nights can be extremely long when I have to wait.

I very reluctantly agreed to Jenna's suggestion to wait until morning to meet with all my Hunters to discuss the journals. Each of them is taking turns watching Tania and helping her through the withdrawals. Apparently, they don't trust me alone with her, and there's no way I'm allowing Sam to be alone with her. So, you have two vampires who don't need sleep waiting impatiently for morning and six humans who could use all the sleep they can get, taking turns staying awake. It's a messed-up situation.

I know I could easily read the journals myself, and I seriously consider doing just that. Sam, on the other hand, has different ideas. Leave it to a man to find having a jealous girlfriend sexy.

"Come back to me."

Sam's husky voice brings me out of my reverie, and I turn my attention back to him.

"Sorry, baby. I'm just so ready for all of this to be over."

I understand, Anala. But for now, let's just see this time we share as the gift it is. Tomorrow will come soon enough.

I know Sam is worried about what's coming. Honestly, so am I. Things definitely aren't as they seem here, and until I learn everything we need to know, I don't believe my Hunters are safe. Damn it. If only all of this could have ended with Thomas. Sadly, I can't keep blaming this on Thomas or even Bernard. We need to discover who our real enemy is this time. Is it Malcolm? The Priestess? Tania?

"Help me take my mind off everything. Just for a few hours," I beg Sam. I realize that when Sam pulls me into his strong arms, nothing soothes me more than the love and security I feel right here in his embrace.

CHAPTER SEVEN
"MY FAMILY."

"How's Tania?"

"Still alive," Jenna answers. "Were you hoping for a different answer?"

I shoot Jenna a death glare before pointedly ignoring her. "Any more complications?" I ask Amanda.

"Not really. A few more gross moments, but once we got her to go to sleep, it was fine."

"Is she still sleeping?"

Amanda begins spreading the books across the table while keeping up with my questions.

"Yes. I was prepared to give her a sedative, but I believe she'll be out for a while. We'll each share our thoughts on the journals and then check on her."

Good plan. I'm confident enough in Amanda, and even Jenna, to know that they have caught the others up on what we believe is going on. Even though I am now having second thoughts. I can't help but wonder if it's because of my innate dislike for Tania now, or if my gut is seriously telling me there's something wrong here. I push back that thought for now, nod to Amanda, and pick up one of the journals. "Who's first?"

"I'll go first. I had what looks to be the first in the series," Sara answers. "From what I can tell, the firstborn Anala Lagan is the direct descendant of someone named Emma Lagan."

"Oh God."

"Do you know her?" Emily looks at me curiously. They can obviously figure out that a Lagan would be related to Thomas.

"Emma was Thomas's sister."

The others just stare at me in complete disbelief for a moment. I wonder if they are recalling the story I told them about when I was changed. It was the only time I mentioned Thomas's sister to them. She was young then—maybe nine or ten if I remember right. I find it hard to see Emma as anything but the scared little girl I almost accidentally killed that day.

"But that doesn't explain why Thomas's sister..." Sara begins.

"I think I can shed some light on why she had a daughter and named her Anala," Eric interjects.

We all turn to him expectantly as he opens the second journal. "It says here that Thomas was the only boy," Eric looks up at me for confirmation. When I nod, he continues. "It also states that Emma became the only one who could pass on the Lagan name when Thomas . . . um . . . died."

"But that was unheard of back then," I mutter. "Hell, it's not completely heard of these days."

"Well, we're still going over the journals, and I honestly don't think we have all of them here," Amanda explains. "We're just trying to piece everything together, but we don't know if we have all of the information we need."

"Okay, give me what you have, and we'll go from there."

"Well," Eric begins again. "It seems that Emma took *your* death pretty hard."

"Mine?"

"Yes. She looked up to you. Wanted to be like you. Thomas wasn't the only one who was devastated. But after her brother died, she changed."

"Changed how?"

"She became obsessed with training. She sought out everyone who had trained with you, wanting to emulate you. Emma even trained with two swords."

The dual swords were my trademark. Other Hunters considered the second sword to be unnecessary and bulky. The women especially thought so. However, this doesn't explain *why* Emma became so fixated on me.

"Apparently, Thomas spoke of you often, as did his—or their—parents. You were said to be betrothed to him."

"*What!*" The word bursts from both Sam and me at the same time. Eyes widen as I grab the book from Eric's hands.

"There's no way! My father would *never* just hand me over to someone."

I flip through page after page, not really knowing what I was searching for, but lacking the clear mind to realize it. Betrothed?! Impossible! Then again, I never thought someone named Anala Lagan was possible. Son of a . . .

"Here." Eric calmly turns to the page I was looking for, then sits back silently as I read.

Father told me about the promise of Anala becoming part of our family. It was supposed to give us the recognition we needed to become a ruling family in the Society of Hunters. With the Geils and Lagans coming together, no one would be able to challenge our authority. With Anala gone and now Thomas, it is up to me to keep our legacy alive. Mother and father agree with my plan. Now, all I need to do is find a suitable beau who will not question my motives and hope for a daughter. Thomas was a good enough Hunter, but Anala was the one people would turn to. The one people would fear. A daughter is the only thing that will do. I shall name her Anala and raise her to be as good as her namesake. If she is not, we will try again.

"Why the cloak?" I ask no one in particular, and I'm not surprised when Eric just flips a few pages for me.

The Cloaked One has all but made Hunters irrelevant here in the village. However, Father has told me of other areas plagued by Cursed Ones. Once I have a daughter, we will stay here for training and then move to an area where we can further develop Anala's abilities. The Cloaked One has not been seen in this area for quite some time. I think I will adopt the Cloak for my Anala. It will make her seem more formidable. Those who have heard of the Cloaked One already hold fear in their hearts. I will make sure to keep that fear going. No one will question my daughter's power. They will flock to her for guidance.

This is all too much to take in. My 'namesake' was essentially created to be a ruler. But why?

"Do I want to know how many 'Analas' Emma went through to get to the *one?*"

"That's not in any of the books we have," Jenna answers. "It could be one of the parts that is missing. Or something they didn't want to write about."

I nod distractedly. "Well, now we know where Anala Lagan came from. And why."

"Yes," Amanda agrees. "It makes you wonder if you had known about Cursed Ones in other areas, would this Priestess be relevant now?"

"There's still so much we don't know. And I doubt we'll find the answers we need in these books." I toss the journal back on the table, sitting back with a sigh.

"Do you think the Priestess will talk to you?"

Sam stumbles over the word priestess, and I don't blame him. If I thought the moniker 'The Cloaked One' was ridiculous when I first heard it whispered around, 'Priestess' was twice as bad. So pretentious. I don't understand it. Was she religious? Or did she just have enough ego to believe she 'lorded' over everyone? I think I'll go with the latter if she's anything like her mother sounded.

"I have no idea. Damn it, there's just too much I don't know. Too many variables. I don't know what role Malcolm or Tania play, or how many territories we're talking about." I feel Sam's hand cover mine and gently squeeze. This is all so overwhelming, and I welcome the grounding sensation.

"Do you believe Tania will tell you where to find the Priestess? Or that she even knows?"

I let out a frustrated growl that the others apparently find amusing. Not only do I not know the damn answer to that, but I also don't want to have to depend on Tania for anything!

Sam laughs loudly at the colorful names I call her in my head, while silently agreeing with me. Which, by the way, is damn good judgment on his part.

"We're not even going to ask what she was thinking," Jenna chuckles. "I'm sure if it were about Tania, we could figure it out ourselves."

Well, flirting bitch or not, I need to find out what she knows about Anala Lagan. But I swear, if she gets touchy-feely again, she's going to have to learn how to brush her teeth with her toes.

We decide to get some training in while we wait for Tania to awaken. When Amanda and Jenna had checked on her earlier, she seemed to be doing much better. She still had the sweats and shakes, but at least the nausea had subsided. I take a moment to wonder what could be making her sleep so much. I had expected her to have insomnia, but she can't seem to stay awake. I shrug a little, thinking I really have no idea what withdrawal really looks like since I've never been through it.

"I could totally take your head off right now," Jenna teases, breaking through my thoughts. "You're getting sloppy."

I send her a mock glare, because deep down, I know she's entirely right. I had let my thoughts take over and stopped paying attention to the here and now. *And this is why you're a damn vampire, Anala.*

"Sorry," I mutter.

I feel Amanda come up beside me and lay her hand on my shoulder.

"It's understandable, Ana." She pauses, as if she's waiting for me to blow up. If it were any other time, I might have. They know better. I know better. But here, with my friends, my family, my Hunters, I let my guard down, and they understand why. "I mean, it's not every day you find out you have a namesake out there."

"It's not that," I confess. "Well, not only that." I retract my swords and toss them to the side. I really should treat them better since they're such antiques, I think fleetingly. With a frustrated sigh, I sink to the floor and sit cross-legged.

"Something is going on up here," I point to my head, "and I don't know if it's skewed because of my feelings or not."

"Why don't you tell us? Let us help." Emily says shyly.

"Yeah, you know we're here for you, A," Jeremy concurs.

I smile genuinely at them. It never ceases to amaze me how far we've come in what is essentially a short amount of time. I'm awed by my Hunters every day.

"It's about Tania. Something is really bothering me about her."

"Well, of course, she got all up in Sam's business," Jenna chuckles.

"It's more than that, though that does piss me off," I acknowledge. It would do me no good to deny what is obvious. "When I saw her in the kitchen last night, she asked if Malcolm was dead. When I told her no, she was...shocked. And, if I'm not mistaken, she was not happy with me."

"Well, he was forcing her to be a servant. And, apparently, *she* is supposed to be the, um, ruler of this territory. Maybe she's just tired of him." Sara points out.

"Yeah, I get that. But..."

"But you have a gut feeling that there's more," Sam states, obviously knowing my thoughts, but still needing to hear more about my feelings.

"Yes." I pause, trying to figure out how to voice my feelings without sounding, well, like a jealous girlfriend. "I'm not really sure what I think is going on. Malcolm is apparently planning a coup, but if women are the heir apparent, how did he possibly get control?"

"He overpowered her?" Jeremy suggests.

"Maybe." My agreement is noncommittal. I have my doubts about someone like Malcolm overpowering anyone. Of course, there is Meathead. "Or maybe she wants him to *think* he's in power. What if she's leading him, and his followers, to a slaughter?"

"Can't say I would be sad," Jenna says grumpily. She obviously does not like feeling like a second-class citizen.

"Jenna. I know he's an asshole, but he's also an innocent."

The others snort their disgust, but deep down, I know they recognize the truth.

"Tania can't be the mastermind behind this. I mean, why would she allow herself to be drugged? And why would she want you to kill Malcolm yourself?" Amanda questions.

"Those are the million-dollar questions, aren't they?" I ask in return. "Perhaps the drugging is Malcolm's little game? A punishment for his sister, who is the rightful ruler? He doesn't seem like the type to bow down to what he sees as the weaker sex. I don't understand how Tania couldn't know she was being drugged, but the withdrawals seemed to take her by surprise. I just don't know if she's acting. As for her wanting me to kill Malcolm, I don't think it matters to her who does it, only that it's done." I blow out a frustrated breath. "And I have no idea if I'm making all of this up in my head because the tramp has eyes for my boyfriend."

"Actually, I think it makes perfect sense," Sam says quietly. "There are a lot of holes that we need to fill, but I don't think Tania will do that for us. Especially if she's in on it."

The others nod in agreement, and I find myself letting out a breath of relief. I'm not used to these feelings of self-doubt and insecurity, but I wasn't sure if my gut feeling was being influenced by my personal emotions.

"They can't want to get rid of all male Hunters, can they?" Jeremy asks weakly.

Damn. I had only been thinking that they would want to get rid of those who believed the right to be a leader should be theirs. But what if it's all of the males? I glance over at Jeremy and Eric, then linger on Sam. Not going to happen. I will do whatever it takes to protect what is mine—my family.

CHAPTER EIGHT

"I WANT SAM."

"So, what do we do with Buffy?" Jenna asks with her mouth full of hamburger.

"Must you talk with your mouth full," Emily complains, to which Jenna responds by opening her mouth wide to show everyone her mushy, chewed food.

"You really are a pain in the ass, aren't you," I smirk. Sometimes I marvel at the enigma that is Jenna. As a cheerleader in high school, she was the epitome of popularity. She dressed the part, acted the part, and had the boyfriend. But after spending the last few months with her, I've come to know the real Jenna. Closet geek, kinda gross, and funny as hell. I've decided that I like this Jenna much more than the one she portrayed in school.

"Yep," she grins. "But you haven't answered my question. And you can't say throw her back to the wolves."

"I haven't figured out what to do about her, actually. But we can't do anything until she tells us where the Priestess is."

"Maybe Sara can get the info from her," Amanda suggests. Then, when she sees my confusion, she goes on: "I mean, if she has a...thing for Sam, she may not be as forthcoming with you."

"Fine," I growl. Yes, growl. I can't help it. Just thinking about Tania having feelings for Sam pisses me off. "Sara gets one shot. After that, I compel Tania. I don't have time for her sh..."

45

"She'll go up now," Amanda interrupts, nodding her head at Sara.

I really need to calm down, I know. But with Tania's little infatuation, Malcolm's disregard for women, having to wear these damn contacts that are giving me a headache, and having this unquenchable desire for Sam, I'm a bit crabby.

Sara walks out of Tania's room, closing the door softly behind her.

She says you have to be invited to have an audience with the Priestess," Sara begins explaining. She had been in there for nearly an hour. An hour of me pacing the damned hall, almost forcing myself not to just walk in and take over. And all Sara could get out of the little tramp was I needed to be invited?

The *only* thing stopping me from snapping Sara's head off is the warmth of Sam's hand on the small of my back. I can feel my irritation slowly leaking out.

"And did she tell you *how* to get invited to have an *audience* with this *Priestess*?" Okay, so I still have a bit of irritation that comes out in the form of sarcasm.

"No," Sara answers carefully. "She said she would only tell..."

"Don't tell me. She will only tell Sam?" I'm so glad Sam is cursed right now. Otherwise, I'd definitely be breaking his hand while squeezing the life out of it. Hey, it's either that or totally losing my temper, and no one wants that.

"Actually, you," Sara explains.

"She wants to talk to me?" I don't think I could be more surprised by that. Surely she knows that she is not my favorite person right now. I haven't even tried to make it a secret. "Why?"

"She said she's only allowed to talk to the 'ruler' of a chapter of the Society." Sara shrugs. "She obviously can see you are the leader, so she wants to see you."

Sigh. Now I have to play nice with the tramp.

Do you like me to come in with you? Sam asks wordlessly.

Are you kidding? I need information. If you're in there and she says anything or looks at you funny, I won't get anything from her except blood.

Sam's eyes widen with shock, then he begins to chuckle.

I think I like it when you're jealous.

Soak it up, pal. I've never been a jealous person, but I can't seem to control it when it comes to you.

Sam pulls me close and buries his face in my neck. I shiver as I feel his lips near my ear.

"I don't see a problem with that," he whispers. His hot breath tickles my ear, and I groan as I push him away.

"I need to handle this; don't distract me."

He smirks, and I playfully stick my tongue out at him.

"Keep that in mind for later," he teases. Then, thankfully, he stops tormenting me. It's nice to be able to joke, even if just for a moment. It goes a long way toward easing a lot of the stress I feel building up inside me.

"Hmm. Okay, let's get this show on the road. If you hear screaming, just turn a deaf ear." I'm kidding, of course—a little.

"You wanted to see me?"

Let me just say, it takes a whole lot of willpower to be nice to Tania. I walk purposefully toward the chair next to the window. It's the furthest piece of furniture from her, unless I want to sit on the dresser.

"It is you who wants something from me, no?" she responds, a bit too smug for my taste, and I grip the arms of the chair tighter.

"I believe *you* came to us for help, Tania. Of course, if you disagree, I can take you back to Malcolm."

She blanches for a moment before I see her regain her composure. With a wicked grin, she turns her eyes towards me.

"You could do that, but you wouldn't obtain the information you need."

Her self-satisfied attitude is seriously getting on my nerves, and I imagine ripping her head off and using it as a cup to drink her blood from.

Anala!

Obviously I'm not going to do that, Sam. But she is dangerously trying my patience.

I understand, baby. Just get what you need and get away from her. Your whole demeanor changes when you're around her. I can feel it.

I pause to think about that. He's right. I become somewhat of a monster when I'm around her. I know it started when she showed her interest in Sam. So... I'm a green-eyed monster. Fantastic.

"Fine," I concede. "I've provided you shelter and protection from Malcolm. You are right to assume that I am the Leader here. In exchange for what I've given, I want information about the Priestess and where to find her."

There. Clear and direct. Any leader who values what that power provides would accept that offer.

"An audience with the Priestess is worth more than shelter," she snaps. I note that she conveniently left out protection.

"What do you want, Tania?" I ask angrily.

"It is customary in these parts to give a gift to the Ruler who grants passage to the Priestess."

I stare at her, dumbfounded. What more could she possibly want? Of course, I know that she wanted me to kill Malcolm, but I can't imagine she would hold that over me for this information.

"What do you want?" I ask again.

"I want Sam."

What happened next was a little fuzzy. It felt like it took place in slow motion, but at the same time, it went by so quickly. All I really remember is seeing red because of Tania's request. I couldn't stop the change even if I wanted to, and I'm not sure I did want to. I wanted to tear her apart. All I could think about was sinking my teeth into her and ripping her throat out, drinking her dry.

One moment I was reaching for Tania - her eyes wide with shock and fear - and the next, Sam was holding me back, whispering soothing words in my ear. Amanda, Jenna, and Sara were immediately at Tania's side. Whether they were holding her back or keeping me from attacking her, I don't know. I sense the others waiting outside the door, and I can't help but wonder if they're prepared to kill me if I get past Sam. The thing is, I don't want to get past Sam. I want to stay here in his arms and let everything else fade away.

But now I have the problem of Tania knowing what I am. She's a Hunter. I'm Cursed. I'm not afraid for my life; I'm afraid for hers. If I can't calm down, she's in serious danger from me.

"I've never felt this way, Sam. Not even when I found out that Bernard had my parents murdered." I shiver and try to calm myself by focusing on the random patterns Sam is gently stroking on my back. "Not even Thomas made me feel this way. The last time I felt this on edge was when I thought you..."

"Shh. I'm here. I've got you."

She...she actually wants me to hand you over to her," I laugh at how utterly ridiculous it all is. If I don't laugh, I'm afraid I might just go a little insane right now. "Is she insane? This Priestess stuff means nothing. Nothing!"

"You know we can't let this continue. There are too many killings happening. We have to regulate this."

I push away from him angrily. Not believing what I am hearing.

"Are you saying you want me to give in to her request!?"

"No! Of course not. You know nothing could ever separate me from you." Sam steps to me, taking me in his arms again. "She saw you, baby. We have to do something about that."

My eyes snap up to meet his gaze. I stare intently, trying to decipher what he means. Knowing my Sam, he can't mean to kill Tania.

Not kill her. He assures me silently. *Though if it came to either you or her...*

He let the statement end there, though I know instinctively what he wanted to say. I steal a glance at Tania, who is still wide-eyed, clearly in shock. Amanda, Jenna, and Sara still surround her. I realize then that they're not protecting her from me but holding her back from running. When Eric, Emily, and Jeremy peek in the door, their eyes immediately lock on Tania. It occurs to me that they're not there to keep her safe from me. They trust me completely, and they'll do whatever it takes to protect me. Too bad I don't trust myself.

I have to compel her. I tell Sam, and he nods his head. *I don't know if I can.*

"Why?" he asks aloud, his eyes confused.

"What's going on?" Amanda asks from the bed, her hand securely on Tania's shoulder.

"Sh-she's..." Tania raises a hand accusingly and points at me.

"Shut it, Buffy," Jenna grouses, pushing Tania's arm down.

Tania looks at her, horrified. "How could you? You're just like Malcolm! Real followers of the Priestess do *not* associate with *them*!"

"Huh. Good thing we don't follow the Priestess. We follow her," Jenna remarks snidely, jerking her chin towards me.

Any other time, I would have taken a moment to revel in a Jenna compliment (because that's certainly how I took it). I just don't have a moment.

"Find a way to keep her quiet and here. I need to talk to all of you," I order and march out of the room. I need to put some distance between myself and Tania before I do something I might regret.

CHAPTER NINE

"JUST HOLD ON."

A s I pace around the mediation room, I'm acutely aware of the irony that the room, which is meant to soothe, feels like a cage to me.

"Baby, you need to calm down," Sam soothes. "C'mere." He holds out his arms, and I immediately fall into them, welcoming the strength.

"I know I'm being stupid," I begin.

"Not stupid," he assures me. "She knows perfectly well that we're together. If anyone is being foolish, it's her."

"Hmm," is my noncommittal answer. Truth is, I feel foolish. I feel like a damn teenager and not a six-hundred-plus-year-old vampire that has been through so much in the past centuries. I've lived through losing my parents, plagues, wars... and the one thing that brings me to the brink of losing myself is jealousy.

Actually, it's me.

Sam's voice in my head startles me out of my reverie.

"What?"

"Jealousy isn't what's causing you to feel out of control. It's me," he states quietly. When I gaze into his eyes, I see the different emotions he's struggling with. Love, loyalty... guilt. Guilt?

I place my palms on his face and gently stroke his cheeks with my thumbs. "Why do you feel guilty, baby?"

"I'm not sure." He tries to turn away, but I hold him closer and wait patiently for him to continue. "Your humanity is in jeopardy because of me."

"That's not true."

"Sure it is. Before me, you had control. You had..."

"Nothing," I finish for him. "I was ready to die, Sam. This life, this *never-ending* life had become too . . . lonely. I've watched people die all around me. I never let anyone close enough to feel *anything* because I couldn't handle it anymore. *That* is what was making me lose my humanity, baby."

I gently pull his head down and kiss him softly on the lips.

"We'll work on this jealousy thing. Actually, we need to work on the amazing connection thing that's going on. It's wreaking havoc on my senses."

Sam chuckles lightly. "Mine, too. Luckily for me, I'm not dealing with someone else trying to get with you since..." his voice trails off, and I know he was thinking of Zac. He pulls me into a hug, holding on tight until we are interrupted by the others pushing their way into the room.

"Okay, we got the... are we bothering you?" Jenna comments sarcastically when Sam and I break apart abruptly.

"Where is Tania?" I ask, ignoring her question.

"We sedated her," Amanda answers tentatively. "And kinda sorta tied her to the bed."

Laughter kinda sorta bursts out of me at that visual. "Well, at least we don't have to worry about her getting away and telling the Priestess that I'm a vampire," I say. "Let's sit." I gesture to the pillows that litter the floor and try to find the words to explain to them what my dilemma is.

"The feelings are too strong for you, aren't they?" Emily asks, surprising me with her perception.

"Yes."

"Wait, what does that mean?" Jenna asks, leaning back on her hands and crossing her ankles in front of her.

"It means that if I try to compel Tania, I may kill her," I answer factually.

"Oh my God, seriously?" Amanda leans closer to me, taking my hand in hers. "How? I mean, would you be telling her to kill herself?"

"No! You know me better than that, Amanda."

"If I may?" Eric addresses the room and continues when I nod. "When you compel someone, you're using the power of your mind to control theirs, correct?"

"Mmhmm."

"With Ana's feelings towards Tania, she could override her brain, possibly, um..."

"Frying it?" Jenna suggests with a smirk.

"Essentially," I admit.

"What about Sam?" Sara proposes.

"No!" My answer is too harsh, and I wince before apologizing. "First of all, that would be putting Sam in danger by exposing what he is to Tania. Second, he has no experience with compelling."

"I could try," Sam offers.

"I don't want you near her, Sam."

"We need the information, baby. If there's a chance I could get that, we need to take it," Sam tries reasoning.

I stand abruptly and start pacing. I know we need the damn information, but I do not want Sam near Tania. I'm not sure I can control myself if she tries something with him. Sure, he doesn't have experience, but I know from experience that compulsion is easy for us. It doesn't take much practice, but there's no reason for Sam to know that — and I shouldn't have had that thought. Damn it.

"So, I *could* do it," Sam says aloud.

"If you're going to listen in on my thoughts, Sam, listen to them all. Don't pick and choose what you want to hear," I chide.

"I did listen. I just have more faith in you than you seem to have," he shoots back.

"Okay, can someone please fill in us non-mind readers here? It's like walking in on a conversation that we missed the beginning of," Jenna complains.

Sam sighs when I stay quiet. "She knows I can compel Tania, but is afraid she would try killing her if she tried anything with me."

"Tried anything?" Jeremy asks. "Like kiss you?"

Jeremy's mouth snaps shut audibly at my feral growl. The thought of Tania's lips on Sam sends such an intense surge of rage through me that my knees weaken. Sam immediately moves to my side, panting lightly. When I turn my curious gaze to him, I feel his mind open completely to mine. He senses the rage I feel, and I can actually experience the virtual tug-of-war between his humanity and the rage.

"*Leave*," I whisper, keeping my eyes fixed on Sam. I desperately hope that Amanda understands, and I feel immense relief when she gathers everyone and quickly ushers them out the door. If I don't get a handle on these issues with Tania, Sam could be in serious danger.

"I'm sorry," I murmur close to his ear. "Hold on to me, baby. Just hold on."

Sam holds on to me tightly, trembling. *What's happening?*

I hear the panic, and it makes me wince.

"You're feeling my anger towards Tania. I think it's more than you expected. Maybe more than you can handle right now."

Sam lifts his head to look me in the eye. "You don't think I'm strong enough?"

"No, baby, it's not that. It's just that we haven't had the chance to deal with all of this."

"You're still waiting for me to lose it?"

Sigh.

I take a moment to consider the answer to that question. "No, I'm not, actually. But I'm struggling with these emotions. I can't imagine you're not."

"It's difficult," he admits. "I don't want either of us around her any longer than we have to be. So, we need to hurry and get what we need from her."

"I know. I just don't like how we have to do it."

"So, you're really going to let Sam..."

Jenna stops when Amanda elbows her in the side, shaking her head. Jenna shrugs but gives me a contrite look. I think even she can tell I'm too stressed out for jokes right now. It took another thirty minutes to calm both me and Sam down after my little outburst (and I won't get into how we managed to do that). But now I can feel myself getting tense all over again.

"Ana, is Sam ready for this?" Amanda asks gently.

"I hope so," I answer distractedly.

"Maybe he should practice," she suggests. "I mean, it would probably be best if he tried with one of us before going in there."

It's a good idea. I should have thought of it. But I'm not so arrogant that I can't accept the help when I need it.

"Are you volunteering?" I ask teasingly.

"Yes. I mean, I am his sister. I suppose I can put my mind in his hands. So to speak," she smiles.

"You sure you want to do that?" Sam teases as he walks up, slinging an arm around Amanda's shoulders. "You never know what I might compel you to do. Maybe quack like a duck? Bawk like a chicken?" He grins.

God help me, but that grin does stuff to me. I watch, captivated, as Sam's grin widens when he looks at me. I shake my head, trying to clear it of the images of what Sam and I did less than an hour ago. Damn, I am so glad I can't blush.

Sam chuckles at my obvious embarrassment before turning his attention back to Amanda, who punches him lightly in the arm for teasing her.

"You wouldn't!" She dares.

"Nah. I'd just make you yell out dirty words when I give a certain command."

It's my turn to chuckle when Amanda glares mockingly at Sam. I appreciate this brief escape from the seriousness of what's happening around us. I accept it as a gift, feeling the knot in my stomach loosen slightly.

"Alright, children. Let's get on with this so we can figure out what to do with...Buffy, as Jenna so affectionately calls her," I playfully scold, placing my hands on my hips a la Amanda.

Jenna snorts with laughter, causing the rest of my Hunters to join in.

"Ana is right. The sooner we get what we need from Tania, the sooner we can figure out what's going on and get the hell out of here," Emily announces, shocking us with her assertiveness as well as the expletive. Okay, so hell isn't much of an expletive, but for Emily it is.

"You don't find my homeland to be inviting, Emily?" I can't help but tease the small Asian girl. After what happened with Zac, my relationship with Emily has been somewhat strained. Even though I don't blame her for trying to kill me, she still feels guilty, and that makes her even more timid around me.

"No! I mean, yes. I mean . . . "

"I'm teasing you, Emily," I laugh. "I don't find it very inviting at the moment myself. But maybe after all of this, I can show you guys around. It really is beautiful when there aren't homicidal weirdos walking around."

Emily smiles tentatively at me, then allows her smile to broaden when I grin and wink at her.

"Ready?" Sam asks Amanda. I can sense his hesitation to bring up the stress again, but he knows it's time to get back to the task at hand.

CHAPTER TEN

"ARE YOU CRAZY!?"

"Alright, think about what you want Amanda to do," I instruct Sam close to his ear. He nods slightly, indicating he has the thought in his head. I almost laugh aloud when I hear the idea, but I manage to keep a straight face. "Now look into Amanda's eyes and project that thought to her. Make her think it's her idea."

Sam concentrates, staring deeply into Amanda's eyes. I'm surprised that Sam wants to try this silently. It's more challenging, especially for those who have just been turned. But quickly, I see Amanda's pupils start to dilate. In a daze, she stands up, turns toward Jenna, and gives the startled blonde a bear hug. The look on Jenna's face says it all. I can't hold back my laughter, and the others quickly join in with loud guffaws. Jenna glares at me, and I give her my most innocent look.

"I didn't do it!" I told her, pointing at Sam, who looks away and whistles. I laugh harder until tears streak down my face.

"Can you tell her to stop now?" Jenna grouses.

"Say please," Sam smirks.

"Please," she snarls, trying to push a clinging Amanda away from her.

"Release her, baby," I laugh.

"How?" he asks, still snickering at Jenna.

"You have to make sure you're looking into her eyes and tell her you release her," I tell him, guiding him around to Jenna's back so he can see Amanda's comically giddy expression as she hugs an increasingly annoyed Jenna.

"Amanda." Sam's voice cracks with laughter, and he clears his throat. "Amanda, I release you."

Amanda blinks, her brows furrowing as she pushes away from Jenna. "What the hell?"

When she realizes what Sam just made her do, Amanda's face flushes a deep red. Whether it's from embarrassment or anger, I don't know. Maybe both, as she turns to Sam and gives him an earful.

"You sorry piece of . . ." Amanda doesn't finish her thought, but she begins pounding on Sam's chest. Now, maybe if Sam weren't Cursed, I'd be a little surprised by Amanda's reaction, but since I know she can't actually hurt him, I just hide my smile. "You made me hug Jenna?! Jenna?! Are you crazy?? Why the hell would you make me hug her?!" she shouts, pointing angrily at Jenna just to make sure Sam knows who she's talking about.

"You think I liked it?" Jenna asks an angry Amanda. "I could have happily lived my life without that happening."

Amanda ends her tirade at Jenna's snide remarks. "Oh, whatever. You know you liked it." And to my utter shock and amazement, she winks and blows a kiss at Jenna.

I don't know whose eyes were bigger, mine or Jenna's. It isn't until I see the mirth in Amanda's eyes that I start laughing again. Jenna finally sees the hilarity of the situation, and as she does, she snorts her laughter.

Everyone agreed I shouldn't go into Tania's room with Sam. And by that, I mean they said majority rules, and I was to follow their vote. It's okay. I can see it going terribly wrong if I go with Sam. Instinctively, I know she's going to think I've given in to her demands and am handing Sam over to her. The thought of that alone pisses me off. So, I've agreed to stay out, but I'm not stupid enough to let Sam go in alone.

I sent Jenna in with him. What? Disagree with my decision? Think she's still pissed enough by Sam's prank that she would let something happen to him? Oddly enough, I trust Jenna completely when it comes to doing the right thing by me (and Sam). Weird, I know. Plus, there's no love lost between Jenna and Tania, and she could knock her out if need be. A part of me hopes there's a need.

Even though I trust both Sam and Jenna, I keep my attention on what's going on in Sam's mind. I can hear everything being said through the door because of my hypersensitive hearing, but I want to ensure Sam's emotions remain calm. I turn my attention to what's happening inside the room and inside Sam's mind.

"Wake her." Take a deep breath. Calm yourself while waiting for Jenna to obey. I need to steady myself. I can do this. I've been a cop for years and have handled much worse scumbags than Tania. But Tania irritates me more than anyone ever has. I know it's because of how she affects Anala, but I have to push down my emotions and get this done. Anala is counting on me. "Hello, Tania." I try to stay polite as she opens her eyes and focuses on me. Ugh. Don't let her look bother you, don't dwell on it, don't dwell on it.

"She actually did it." I wonder if she thinks that's a seductive smile she's giving me. Crap. Don't think about it. Anala, I love you.

"Did what?" I know what she's talking about, but I need her relaxed enough not to think something is wrong when I get closer.

"She gave you to me." That look gives me the heebie-jeebies.

Uh oh. Baby, calm down. I've got this under control. Please just trust me. If you get upset, it'll only upset me.

"Actually, I'm here to ask you some questions." Okay, she's frowning now. But at least Anala is calmer.

"She thought she could send you in here to get information for her? It doesn't work like that, love."

Damn, damn, damn. Baby, please!

"Tania." Do I risk sitting near her? Yes. Just concentrate on what you need to do. Come on, Sam. Get what you need and get out. *"I need you to tell me where to find the Priestess."*

Baby, I'm concentrating, but it feels like she's trying to push me out.

Push harder.

Damn. Just hearing your voice makes me...

Sam.

Sorry. Concentrating.

"Tell me where to find the Priestess, Tania."

"Are you...mine?" Okay, so her voice is faltering. Does that mean she's weakening? Why is this more difficult than Amanda?

Amanda wasn't trying to resist you. She is. You have to fight harder. Push harder. If she still fights you, you will have to turn.

"You want to tell me where the Priestess is, Tania." Harder. I can practically feel my thoughts drilling into hers. She's wavering.

Just keep eye contact. Push the thought.

"She..."

She's shaking her head; she has to be losing her grip on her resistance. Push harder!

"She is in the original village."

"Original village?"

"Anala's village. There is... a...secluded place."

"Can you show me on a map?"

"It's not on a map."

"Landmarks?"

"Who are you? What are you? What are you doing to me?"

That's enough. Get out of there. Tell Jenna to put her back under for now.

"God, I'm glad that's over."

I watch Sam shake his entire body like a duck shaking off water.

"Me, too," I murmur, pulling him into my arms. "I'm sorry I almost lost it."

"Understandable, baby. But you did great and helped me."

My eyes flutter closed when he tucks a strand of my hair behind my ear. I take a moment to mourn the fact that we can't just stay like this. I resent the fact that after centuries of being alone, when I finally find someone to love, my life is too hectic to enjoy it. Sam's arms tighten around me, and I know he hears my thoughts. My Hunters intuitively know that I need this quiet moment with Sam and say nothing. With a deep breath, I break away from the embrace and give everyone a grim smile. It's time to get this show on the road.

"Alright. First on the agenda is finding where this secret hideaway is," I announce with a bit of trepidation.

Amanda steps toward me, placing a hand on my forearm. "Are you going to be okay going back there?"

I haven't been back to my village since my parents' murder. Will I be okay going back? I don't know. I don't think I have any other choice. Is it ironic that the 'Priestess' chose that place for her residence? Or was it by design considering who her ancestor is?

"Baby?"

"Yes. I'll be fine. I have to be," I answer firmly. "We can't afford for me to be emotional. Any more than I already am," I finish with a mutter.

"And what do we do with Tania?" Jenna asks. I'm slightly concerned by the lack of her sarcasm. What happened with the 'Buffy'?

"Come. Let's get something to eat and discuss. You guys are going to need all your strength, and I haven't been taking the best care of you."

"That's not true. You always make sure we eat," Eric interjects.

"No," I disagree gently. "You always make sure *I* eat. I am your leader, and yet it seems you're taking better care of me than I am of you."

"We're a family, Ana." Amanda squeezes my arm where her hand still rests. "We take care of each other. We knew it would be difficult for you to be here. So, if we have to pick up a little of your slack, that's fine," she says with a teasing smile.

I do what any mature Leader of the Society of Hunters would do. I stick my tongue out at her.

We're gathered around our favorite meeting spot: the dining room table, which just happens to be packed with Chinese takeout. What? Were you expecting fish and chips? I grab the spare ribs away from Jenna before she devours them all.

"Hey! It's not like you need to eat!" she pouts.

"So?" I shrug, my mouth full of spareribs. "Doesn't mean I don't like 'em."

The others chuckle at us, and Jenna flips me off. I roll my eyes playfully and shove the ribs over to her.

"Thanks!" she beams.

"Did anyone happen to take food to our 'guest'?" I ask nonchalantly. If it were up to me, I would let her starve. Good thing it's not up to me since Sara nodded.

"I took her some soup and a sandwich," she confirms. Well, at least the tramp isn't getting any of this good Chinese food.

"Fine. Thank you. I suppose we need to discuss what to do with her." I sip from my 'Hunter' laced bottle of blood, passing it to Sam. If any of my group finds our sharing such a delicacy disturbing, they don't show it. And for that, I'm incredibly grateful.

"Can't we just drop her off in the woods she found us in?" Jenna asks, slurping lo mein noodles from her chopsticks.

I'm about to answer the rudeness that is Jenna when a fortune cookie sails through the air and catches her on the forehead. Let me just say, it takes a great amount of effort not to spew the contents in my mouth out of my nose at that moment (good thing since that would have been kinda gross). Howls of laughter fill the air, and despite everything that is going on, it feels good. No. It feels *amazing* to hear these kids laughing and having fun in defiance of everything they've been through and the things they've had to do. So, I will grant them this time and let them be the young kids they deserve to be.

"If you children are done playing around," I bellow in mock annoyance, "we have a problem to solve!" I catch the flying fortune cookie that was on its way to my face, breaking it open with a flourish. *"You display the wonderful traits of charm and courtesy,"* I read aloud. "Huh. This one certainly doesn't belong to you, Jenna."

"Har har har." She snorts. God, I really think these people are starting to grow on me. I feel - and let - the genuine smile spread across my face before sobering again.

"Seriously, I'm asking all of you for your opinions on what to do with Tania. I don't trust myself to make a rational decision."

"What options do we really have?" Emily asks. I can practically see the genuine concern in her eyes. She can't seriously think we would hurt her, right?

"Could you erase her memory?" Jeremy inquires, picking food out of a container in front of Jenna. I find it quite telling that Jenna does not attempt to move it out of his way. As a matter of fact, she scoots it closer to him. Aww.

"Hunters are harder to maintain a hold over," I tell them, remembering the time I tried compelling Sam. It didn't last very long, and when he came out of it, he was not a happy camper. Of course, he was wary of me. My, how times have changed.

"But Zac was totally taken over," Jenna points out, not unkindly.

"I have to believe Zac was a little off balance," I say gently, hoping not to offend them. "Perhaps it was his unrequited feelings. He was angry, and that diminished his defenses."

"You don't think Tania is 'off balance'?" Sara challenges. "With the drugs and her hatred towards her brother? And you?"

"You have a point," I capitulate. "I know she fought Sam's compulsion, but if I change, perhaps I could break through any defenses."

"Aren't you afraid you'll fry her brain?"

I turn my attention to Amanda and see the concern. Strangely enough, I think her concern is for my humanity more than for Tania.

"If she is sedated, gagged, and Sam's not in the room, I may be able to hold on to my anger." I grin and wink at her.

CHAPTER ELEVEN
"CURSED SLAVES."

"Is she sedated?" I pace nervously up and down the hallway in front of Tania's door. I'm really hoping I don't kill the tramp. I'm not sure I would be devastated if it *did* happen, but it wouldn't look good to my Hunters. Jenna nods at me, her eyes following me as I move restlessly. "Good. Gagged?"

"Yes, she's bound and gagged all 50 shades like," Jenna says, a hint of a smirk creasing the corners of her mouth.

That stops me in my tracks. "That's gross."

"But funny," she adds dryly.

"Whatever," I mutter, squaring my shoulders. "Okay. I'm going in."

"Whatever you do, don't make it a red room." Jenna snorts at her own joke while I fight the urge to groan.

"Broaden your horizons, Jenna. Read something with a little more substance," I tell her, bumping her shoulder as I walk by her.

I pause at the door to catch my breath and make sure my emotions are in check before I attempt to face Tania. The last person I hated was Thomas, and look what I did to him. He also tried to take Sam from me. I can see a trend.

"Can you hear me?" I ask Tania as I approach her. Her eyes are glazed over from the sedation, her hands are tied together, and she has duct tape over her mouth. I briefly wonder where the hell my Hunters got duct tape, then let it go and focus on my task. Tania nods her head, and I note the fear in her eyes. I pull a chair over, sitting close enough to her bed that my knees touch the edge. I made a point of taking my contacts out before I came in, and I wonder what she's thinking as she looks at me.

"I want you to listen to me carefully. You have no idea who you were dealing with when you challenged me. You came to us, asking for help. We did that, and you basically spat in my face for it."

She nods, her eyes cast downward in what I interpret as shame. Whether it's genuine or not, I don't know. And I don't care.

"You have no idea how badly I want to kill you right now," I say, my contempt spilling out like bile. Tania's eyes widen, clear shock and terror shining brightly. "You should never have shown interest in Sam. He is mine. He will always be mine. But you did. And now you've pissed off the one person you never wanted to piss off."

I close my eyes, letting the change take hold. I welcome the burning in my eyes, the ache in my teeth. I feel the power flowing through my veins, and for the first time in a long while, I savor that power. It almost seems as if a soothing balm is being poured over my heart. That thought is a little unsettling, but I push it aside as I look up at Tania. Her fear and shock double, and her eyes become comically large.

"You're really regretting your choices now, aren't you?" I taunt her. I know I shouldn't, but I can't help myself. She pleads with her eyes to talk. "No. You've said quite enough. Now, you get to listen to me."

I lean in closer, holding her gaze.

"You're going to forget that you ever met us. You don't know me or what I am. You don't know Sam. You don't know my Hunters." I turn up the intensity. "You've never been here. You never told anyone about the Priestess. You will *never* remember any of this. This memory has been erased."

Tania's eyes completely glaze over before she closes them, letting her head fall back onto the pillow. Within seconds, she was asleep. I take that opportunity to make my departure.

"Take her back into the forest. Make sure she has warm clothes and something to eat. If she doesn't go back to Malcolm, then maybe she'll lead us to the Priestess. I'll need a team to stay near her but out of sight while the rest of us go to my village." I walk out of Tania's room and immediately assume my leadership role, giving out orders. When no one responds to my demands, I stop and face them with an eyebrow raised in question.

"Are you going to stay that way?" Jenna asks, looking at me curiously.

My eyebrows raise higher into my hairline. "Stay what way?"

"All 'hulked' out."

Damn. I didn't even realize I was still in Cursed mode. How strange. That's never happened to me before. I feel so relaxed. Usually, being like this makes me feel...well, unnatural. I glance at Sam, who has the most curious, serene smile.

"Sorry," I murmur, forcing myself to return to what they recognize as normal. I don't allow myself to wonder why I didn't see it as normal at that moment. "Better?"

"Actually, I think we all kinda dig the 'hulked-out' look," Jenna teases. "But this is cool, too."

"Yes, well, let's suit up and get Tania out of here before she wakes up. Sara, I want you on the team that sticks close to Tania. She seemed to relate to you the most. And even though she won't remember who you are, if something happens and you're noticed, perhaps you'll be able to convince her to take you to the Priestess."

Sara nods intensely. "I'll get her stuff together. Maybe we can give her some money. Obviously we won't be able to give her enough food to last her long if she doesn't go back to Malcolm. But money may help along the way."

"Good thinking. We'll do that. I'll give you enough to cover her for at least a couple of weeks."

"Damn, can I get in on that?" Jenna grins slyly.

I slant an annoyed glance at her. "Jenna, you are traveling in style, eating like a freakin' queen, and I just bought you a butt load of high-end computer equipment. You've gotten in on that."

Jenna holds her hands up in mock surrender without another word.

"Amanda..."

"Sam should be with you, Ana," she interrupts before I can say anything more. "Emily and Eric will go with you. Jenna, Jeremy, and I will stay with Sara. If we see that she is going back to Malcolm, we will catch up to you. If it turns out otherwise, we will stay with her to see where she goes."

I blink. Then, I blink again. It was exactly what I was about to suggest, but hearing Amanda confidently spell out what she thought we should do made pride swell inside me. I see the proud grin Sam has as well as he puts his arm around his little sister.

"Good plan," I say, truly impressed. "Everyone else on board with that?"

I'm met with affirmations from everyone as they pat a blushing Amanda on the back.

"Jenna bought nifty little devices for us to stay connected. With my money, I might add." I wink at a sheepish Jenna. "Let's get suited up and wired. We need to head out as soon as possible. I don't want Tania to wake up in a place she's not supposed to remember."

Amanda, do you copy?" Okay, so I feel a little silly with my terminology, but it seems to entertain my Hunters. 'So covert,' they say. With our dark clothing, earpieces, and moving around in the dark of night, my group is definitely having a good time. I know that when the situation calls for it, they are all business, so I have no problem letting them have their little moments.

"Loud and clear, Selene."

I hear giggles in the background and roll my eyes.

"Did you just call me Selene? As in Underworld?"

"Um. Yes."

"Well...I suppose if I have to be compared to a fake vampire, Kate Beckinsale is a good choice. She was pretty badass in that movie." I pause, tapping my teeth in thought. "Well, since Buffy is already taken, can I call you, um, Van Helsing? Or maybe Abe Lincoln?"

I hear Amanda chortle in my ear before clearing her throat. "Let's stick with Beckinsale movies. I can't be sure about the authenticity of Abe Lincoln being a Hunter."

Amanda says it so seriously that my burst of laughter fills the quiet inside the car, causing the other occupants to look at me with curiosity.

"Fine, Van. We're about one hundred kilometers from my village. Has Buffy risen yet?"

"Yep. But she has yet to do anything. She seems to be groggy and confused. If she's not going back to Malcolm, she's going to have to find transportation."

"Yes. I'm almost tempted to have you pick her up as a hitchhiker. Is your car secure?"

"Yes, and we're not far from it in case we need to make a fast getaway."

"Good. Any problems?"

"Nope, it's eerily quiet. I was expecting some distractions, but so far, nothing."

"Hmm. That's disturbing."

"I know. I mean, you would think our buddy Malcolm would have his little Cursed slaves roaming around."

"Cursed slaves," I repeat slowly.

"Sorry, Ana!" Amanda whispers vehemently. "I didn't mean anything..."

"What happened to Selene?" I interrupt teasingly, trying to squelch Amanda's remorse, and I immediately hear a sigh of relief.

"Right, my bad. Okay, Sleeping Buffy is getting ready to move out. I'll keep you updated. Keep this line open. Van Helsing out."

I chuckle at Amanda's silliness. "Tania is moving. Don't know where, yet," I tell the others. "There are no Cursed around."

"That's odd," Sam comments distractedly, gazing out of the side window.

"Perhaps it's because they're missing the others from when we went to Malcolm's to get the journals," Eric suggests.

"Yes," Emily agrees. "They have no accounting for the others or what happened to them. If they're planning something with the Priestess, won't they need all the help they can get from their..."

"Cursed slaves," I offer. Emily shrugs timidly. The demure gesture has me thinking of what an enigma Emily is as well. When she is fighting, she is a force to be sure. Don't let her tiny stature fool you; the girl can kick ass. But when she puts her sword down, her entire demeanor changes. She retreats into herself and becomes shy and quiet.

"You may be right," I allow. I brief Amanda on Eric and Emily's theory. She agrees and proceeds to tell me that Tania is not heading towards Malcolm's.

I find myself surprised by Tania's decision. I wouldn't have expected her to have much genuine internal strength. She isn't a leader - or ruler - she's a follower. However, I suppose she's choosing to follow the Priestess instead of her brother.

"Tania has made her decision. The others are about an hour and a half behind us."

"She's going to the Priestess?" Sam inquires.

"Seems so. She's headed in this direction."

"Transpo?"

"She's walking at the moment, but obviously she can't walk all the way. We'll see what she does."

Sam nods, turning his attention back to what's beyond the window.

Are you okay?

Sam glances at me with a small smile.

Yes. Just thinking.

His answer surprises me because I haven't heard any thoughts. Of course, I've been preoccupied myself, but I can't imagine I would be so out of touch with Sam.

Are you shutting me out? I ask incredulously.

Sam turns to me sharply. *No! I don't know how to do that. I don't want to do that.*

I think about that for a moment. He doesn't know how, but that doesn't mean he didn't do it unintentionally.

Are you worried about how I will feel about whatever you're thinking?

Sam shrugs, then nods. I realize then that he may have just inadvertently figured out how to shut me out.

Sam, baby, let me in.

I'm not keeping you out. I swear.

You're afraid of me. Afraid of my reactions. That is shutting me out of your thoughts.

Sam stares at me for what seems like an eternity.

I'm not afraid of you, Anala. But I admit I am afraid of my thoughts.

Tell me.

Sam closes his eyes and sighs deeply.

I felt something... different when you were changed.

Do you know what it was?

No. Not really. It was just very...

Calming?

Sam's eyes widen.

Yes! I was worried that maybe it indicated my - or our - humanity was failing.

I felt it too. But I don't believe it's our humanity that's failing. Maybe I pause to reflect for a moment. *Perhaps, for the first time, I don't feel... Cursed.*

"Because of me?" Sam asks softly. "Because we're together?"

"Yes."

CHAPTER TWELVE

"THE JOURNEY HOME."

"She's made a stop."

Amanda's voice crackles in my earpiece, startling me. After my and Sam's 'discussion', we both retreat into our own thoughts. But this time, the difference is that Sam is connected to me. He keeps his hand on me constantly, either by placing it on my thigh or holding my hand while gently stroking his thumb over my knuckles.

"Where?" I ask quietly as Eric and Emily are napping in the back seat.

"Residence. Jenna is looking it up now. From what we could see, the occupant is female and seemed to know Buffy pretty well."

"Do you think it's another Hunter?"

"I can't be sure, but gut says yes. I mean, if Buffy is going there, I can't help but wonder if this will be her ride to Anala, Jr....um, or Anala the Hundredth or whatever."

I chuckle at Amanda, watching Sam shake his head with a grin. I know he can hear Amanda just as clearly as I can with his hypersensitive hearing, but I also know he can feel my amusement at Amanda's silliness. It seems we are fully connected again. Sam shrugs sheepishly.

"Okay, we're close to the village. We'll find a place to regroup and wait for you. The twins are asleep, and you guys will need some rest when you get here. I'll give you the info as soon as I have it."

"Gotcha. Are there hotels there?"

"I'm not sure. I guess we'll find out."

"Okay. Ana?"

"Yes?"

"Let Sam help you when you're there. I can't imagine this will be easy for you, so just let him be there for you," she says softly, and I hear her concern loud and clear. I feel truly cared for. Having Sam and Amanda in my life, and even the others who have become an essential part of it, has made me feel things I haven't felt since... well, since my parents.

"I will. I promise."

Sigh. I hate this. The journey home. My apprehension grows as we near my village. Of course, after centuries, it looks completely different. But my feelings are the same as the day I left so long ago. The day I set my childhood home on fire. With my parents inside. Sam squeezes my hand, and I give him a small smile.

Even with Sam beside me, silently supporting me, the pain of the memories threatens to overwhelm me. To my shock, I feel the change begin.

"Baby, stop the car," Sam whispers.

I immediately do as he asks, and he is out of the car and opening my door before I even put it in park.

"Come here." He holds his arms open, and I seek refuge in his strength. "Are you okay?"

I nod, burying my face in his neck and reveling in the unique scent that is my love. With the consoling words being whispered in my ear, I feel myself begin to relax, the change stopping immediately.

"Are we here?" Emily asks sleepily from the back seat, glancing around at... well, nothing since I stopped in the middle of nowhere. "Is everything alright?"

"Yes. Sorry." I murmur, still ensconced in Sam's arms.

"No apologies are necessary, Ana." Eric leans over to peer out the window. "We all had a feeling this would be difficult for you. Take as much time as you need."

If I could see Eric in any profession, it would be as a politician. And I mean that as a genuine compliment. He says all the right things, is diplomatic and level-headed. I have no doubt he would be a good choice for a position of power.

"Do either of you have your phone with you?" I ask, and continue when they both nod. "Could you see if there's a motel or something nearby? You guys could use a bed to sleep in, and we can wait for the others."

"Sure," Emily agrees, pulling her phone out.

"Sam and I will be right back. I just want to take a quick look around."

I grab Sam's hand and lead him into the woods surrounding us.

"Do you think there will be Cursed Ones out here?" he asks, his eyes peering intently into the depths of the trees.

"I don't know. I just needed to do this." I tug Sam to me and kiss him deeply.

Mmm. I'll do that with you anytime and anywhere, baby," he says huskily as we break the kiss.

"There's something else I need."

Sam's eyebrows shoot up, and I punch him playfully in the stomach.

"Not that, you deviant," I smile. "But close."

Maybe he reads my mind. Maybe he sees the need in my eyes. Whatever it is, he bends down and offers me his neck, and my salvation.

"Well. This is...quaint." Eric pushes open the room door to the one and only place to stay here in the village.

I told you. Eric is a total politician since the room we're in is just a tiny broom closet. The good thing is there's no one else around, and we have the place to ourselves. So, we rented four rooms. I think the owners of this 'quaint' little place were a bit stunned but happy to hand over the keys to half of their rooms.

"Isn't it, though?" I murmur. All I can think of is how thin the walls are. Somehow, I doubt Sam and I will have any privacy, which sucks (pun intended) because feeding from Sam definitely makes me...

"Ana?"

I clear my throat as Sam laughs quietly. "Yes, Emily?"

"Have you heard from Amanda?"

"Yes. Assuming Tania is on her way here, they're about thirty minutes out. Why don't you two get some sleep? We'll need to keep eyes on Tania at all times unless she ends up bunking down somewhere."

Eric and Emily nod, and Sam and I leave them to go to the farthest room away.

Sam pushes the door closed and backs me up against it. "Feeding from me makes you what?" he asks gruffly.

"I'm pretty sure you know."

"I want to hear you say it."

"Well, I don't!"

Amanda's voice in my ear startles me so much that I jump the entire distance of the room. Okay, it's only about ten feet, but still.

"Damn it, Amanda!" I put my hand over my heart. If I had any doubts that I had a beating heart before, I definitely don't now.

"It's not my fault you left the line open! And I certainly don't want to hear what goes on between you and my brother!"

"Do you have any updates?" The question comes out harsher than I meant, but she interrupted a nice moment that could have turned into something really special.

"Don't get all grumpy with me. At least you have someone to do stuff with that shouldn't be done over an open line."

I open my mouth to respond, then close it again. She's right. Amanda *finally* got her crush to ask her out, and I totally ruined it for her by recruiting her to the Society.

"Sorry."

There's an awkward silence followed by a soft clearing of a throat.

"According to Jenna's search, Tania's friend's name is Monica McKinney. Nothing scandalous to report about her. She's twenty-four and works for a bank. She's been there since she graduated from high school. No arrests, no tickets. She's an all-around Pollyanna as far as anyone can tell. Jenna says she can hack into her Facebook to see who her friends are, but I doubt that would help us much. They're definitely on their way there. We are close to your village."

"It's no longer my village, Amanda," I tell her softly.

"Ana, a part of you will always be there."

I ignore that and move on with the conversation. "Tell Jenna good job on the search. Do you think Buffy and Willow will visit with the Priestess tonight or find a place to sleep for the night?"

As soon as the question is out of my mouth, I realize that the only place they can sleep is right here where we are. Unless, of course, they know someone in the village. If that's the case, we may get names of some of the other players.

"I'm hoping they sleep, 'cause I'm tired as hell."

I can hear the weariness in Amanda's voice, and it makes me cringe. I need to remember that my Hunters need to rest. Rest, eat, train. It's a simple thing to remember. Why am I having such a hard time with it, who the hell knows?

"Sam and I will meet you and take over. You guys head back to the motel and get some sleep."

"We can stick it out until she…"

"No, Amanda. Eric and Emily are sleeping. You guys need to as well. Tell me how far out you are, and we'll take over the tail as you pass by."

"Is that an order?" Amanda asks haughtily.

"Yes, Ms. Crabby Pants, it is. If you're giving me this attitude, it will only get worse the longer you're awake. I don't need that crap." I make sure I put enough teasing in my voice so she knows I'm kidding with her. At least I hope she does.

"Fine, Selene. We're about twenty minutes out, coming in on the main road."

I chuckle at my 'handle.' "We'll be out there, hidden. I'll signal you when we see you. They may head in our direction since this is the only place to sleep around here. If that's the case, Sam and I will keep watch. If not, we will keep going with them and contact you after you've gotten some sleep."

"Can we be sure you and Sam won't be..."

"Yes!" I laugh. "We *can* control ourselves, you know."

"Sure, you can. And Jenna doesn't pop her damn gum."

"Whatever," I laugh. "I have way more self-discipline than blondie. It's really too bad Buffy was taken. Jenna fills that role perfectly."

I hear Amanda telling Jenna what I said. "She's making a hand gesture. I'll leave it up to your imagination what gesture it is. Now get moving or you're not going to make it."

"Yes, ma'am."

I see headlights," Sam announces. We've been waiting just under ten minutes before seeing the little red Toyota Amanda described to us. Tania and her friend will be in that car, followed by Amanda and the others in a silver Audi Q7. The Audi was a bit of an indulgence I allowed my Hunters. It's not as flashy as the sedan they were looking at, but it could still stand out. Especially out here in the middle of nowhere, but I gave in to their whining and rented the SUV for them anyway. I told them to think of it as their graduation gift. Along with the private jet and free trip to Europe. I know they're here to work and will be in what is potentially extreme danger. That's why these little indulgences are easy for me to make.

"Let's pull in behind them and see where they go," I say to Sam before keying the mic to talk to Amanda. "Van?"

"Heh. Yes, Selene?"

"There's a road about two and a half kilometers..."

"Ana, speak in mileage please."

I sigh but smile and oblige. "A little over a mile and a half, there's a road off to the right. I want you to take that road, then make your way to the motel."

"Roger."

I can't help but laugh at the term. "I thought I was Selene," I tease.

"No, roger, as in got it..." she trails off when she hears my laugh. "You're a brat."

"I know. You have your directions to the motel, right?" I wait for Amanda to answer affirmatively and then continue. "Go to sleep when you get there. I doubt anything will be happening tonight anyway."

"Yes, mother."

I bite back my retort as we pull out behind them at a respectful distance. I doubt Buffy and Willow will be suspicious since Sam and I are following in a black Jeep Cherokee. Somehow I just don't see Tania being smart enough to realize she's being followed. The variable, however, is her friend Monica. I don't know how intelligent or trained this new player is. I hate surprises.

Chapter Thirteen

"Cocky son of a gun."

We follow Tania to a small house not far from our motel. I note the address for Jenna to look up later. Instinctively, I know that the Priestess won't be holed up in this modest little house. Anyone who calls herself a Priestess wouldn't settle for anything that doesn't show her importance.

"More Hunters?" Sam asks quietly.

"Could be." I watch the woman who gets out of the car with Tania. She's average height with fiery red hair, but even from this distance, I can see she's powerful. Definitely a Hunter. Maybe even a very skilled one. The house door opens, and another woman with cropped dark hair runs out to meet them. Another athletic-looking woman, and judging by her height compared to the others she's standing next to, she appears to be about my height. Are they Rulers? "Let's get close once they're inside. It's time to do a little recon."

Sam smiles mischievously. This is Sam's wheelhouse—what he was trained to do. He was good—very good—before I cursed him. Just imagine how he's going to be now. I can't help but feel excited just thinking about watching him in his element.

"Let's get this show on the road," Sam smirks, knowing exactly what I'm thinking—cocky son of a gun.

"So, you just woke up in the forest?" our unknown asks Tania.

"Yes. It was weird. I *feel* weird."

"Weird how?" Monica asks.

It seems like Tania and Monica saved this conversation until they arrived here. Is this unknown just a friend? Or is she someone higher up in the chain of command?

"I'm not sure. It feels almost like I've been drugged," we hear Tania explain.

She must be talking about being compelled.

I nod at Sam's assessment.

Will she be able to remember?

I don't think so. Being drugged by Malcolm, I think she was more susceptible to coercion.

"By Malcolm?"

I don't know, Abby. I honestly don't remember anything about leaving the house or anything else. The last thing I remember is Malcolm talking to his cronies about his plans. Then... nothing. I woke up in the woods.

"Do you remember the plans?" Abby asks.

"I-I think so."

"The Priestess will be pleased. We will request an audience with her tomorrow."

"Do you really think she'll see me?"

I can hear the excitement in Tania's voice. It almost sounds like she's about to meet her idol. Maybe she really is. I feel Sam slip away from me, and I lose focus on those inside.

Where are you going?

Just taking a look around.

Sam.

Relax, baby. This is my element, remember?

He winks at me before turning the corner of the house and disappearing. Damn. It's tough to be in love with a cop/Hunter/Cursed One. Sam laughs softly, and I roll my eyes. Especially one who can read all of my thoughts.

Our Priestess followers finally turn in after planning for the next day. Abby, who is apparently higher up, will be the one requesting a meeting with the Priestess. I have no idea how long it will take for a response to that request, but at least my Hunters will be rested by then and able to keep watch.

For now, Sam and I both feel comfortable enough to leave and head back to the motel. Sam didn't find anything interesting during his exploration around the house—no hidden doors or weapons of mass destruction—but that doesn't mean there's nothing inside. Hopefully, it won't come down to us having to break in. I'd rather just follow them to the Priestess and get the confrontation over.

"You're expecting a confrontation?" Sam asks softly.

"I don't know what else to expect," I answer honestly. "I disagree with the way she's running things."

"As do I, baby..."

"But?"

"But she might have information we can use—details about other Cursed Ones. They appear to be exploiting them for their own benefit."

"By taking out the 'bad guys'?" I ask, giving Sam a sideways glance. "Does that make it okay?"

"Of course not! That's not what I meant. However, we will have to take control of them ourselves if we want to stop them. Because that's what it seems like to me. Like the Priestess has trained them, or..."

"Or is controlling them somehow," I finish for him.

"Right. But how?" He hesitates for a moment. "Are you the oldest of your kind?"

I narrow my eyes at him. I have no idea why my age bothers me. It's silly, really. It's just a number. Experience. It's not like I'm wasting away to nothing. I still look like I'm eighteen. I may not feel it all the time, mentally, but my body is supple and strong. But Sam's question makes me pause. Am I the oldest left? I never knew about the others before, so how can I possibly know if there's one older than me? Stronger than me?

"I don't know," I answer quietly. I really hate surprises. Not knowing what I'm up against makes me feel defensive. How can I protect my Hunters—and myself—if I don't know what I'm up against?

So, they're meeting up with Miss High and Mighty today?" Jenna asks, stuffing her face with blueberry pancakes. Despite being such a small, run-down motel, they have quite the breakfast spread. Or maybe they're just happy to have guests, and this is their way of showing appreciation. Whatever the reason, my Hunters are enjoying it.

Well, the one they met up with here, Abby, is requesting a meet today. When that meet actually happens, we don't know," I answer patiently.

"So, why are we here? Shouldn't we be watching them?" Sara sips her orange juice, peering at me over the rim.

There are times when I look at Sara, I can see her warring with herself. I can only assume she is still trying to decide whether I am fit to be a leader or not. Perhaps the way I do things is not how she would do them. Or maybe she is just having problems with what I am. I realize she is still new to our group, but I am seriously getting annoyed with having to explain myself to her.

"Sara, we have it covered. Sam placed devices around the house so we can keep ears on them. We also have tracking devices on the cars. If they make a move, we'll know it." I try to keep my voice light. I really do. But from the small cringe Sara and the others make, I can tell I failed miserably.

"But we're all here, eating and talking as if nothing is happening. Like we're all on vacation." Okay, so apparently, even though I failed to keep my voice light, Sara isn't ready to back down. "Who is monitoring them?"

Listen, Penelope Cruz, Jenna begins, clearly as pissed as I am about Sara's back-and-forth of trusting me. "All of this stuff is portable." She gestures to the gadget in her ear, then to her phone. "We can eat and pay attention at the same time. Ana knows what she's doing. And just for the record, so do we. So stop your whining and eat your damn pancakes."

I'm smart enough to hold back the laugh that threatens to escape. The look on Sara's face shows it wouldn't be appreciated. But I still can't help finding Jenna's defense of me funny. Not to mention her constant need to call people by anything other than their name.

"At least you chose someone from the correct country," Sara shoots back. To my amazement, she then smirks. "And she's hot, so I'll take the compliment."

This time, I do laugh. The indignant look Jenna gives Sara is too comical not to.

"Alright, *ladies*, and I use that term loosely," Amanda says, looking pointedly at Jenna. "Let's just finish eating and planning. Your bickering is hurting my head."

"Who died and made you leader?" Jenna teases.

"Well," Amanda smiles. "We don't really know if Ana is technically alive..."

"Hey!" I feign pain, holding my hand over my 'bleeding' heart. "Alive or not, I still feel pain," I pout.

"Aww, poor little vampire," Amanda coos. "It's okay. We still love you."

Sam's shoulders shake with uncontrollable, yet silent laughter.

Keep it up, pal. Centuries of living have given me plenty of ideas for torture.

Sam's laughter turns into a mischievous grin. Oh dear.

"There's chatter."

Eric's words make me tear my eyes away from Sam and shake off the feelings I constantly have when thinking of him. Eric holds a finger to his ear. He has the same gadget Jenna has and has been quietly keeping tabs while everyone else ate and argued.

I take out my own earphone and put it in my ear. "Did they say a name?"

Eric shakes his head negatively, then, after looking around to see if we are alone, he plugs his earpiece into a small speaker for everyone to hear. He keeps the volume low, so the others lean in to listen to the soft voices.

"It's Abby. We have a pupil who may have information for the Priestess."

There's a silence, and I imagine she's listening to whoever she's talking to.

"I understand that, but... she is Malcolm's sister. She's heard plans...I don't know... but... yes, Madame. I understand the rules. No, Madame, we have not spoken to anyone else. No, she wasn't followed. Yes, of course. We will be waiting."

There is a distinct click, and soft footsteps before we hear anything else.

"We will be escorted to the Priestess in an hour. You better have something good, Tania. The Priestess does not meet anyone unless it is important. If you have nothing to give her, she will deem you and us as unworthy. Do you understand?"

"She would throw us out? But we are Rulers!" Tania protests.

"No, she will not throw us out. If you prove unworthy, she has no use for us. She will kill us."

"Damn. I bet you're liking Ana as a leader right about now, huh, Sara?"

Sara's face pales, which isn't easy with her dark complexion. Her eyes drift to mine, and I see her fear. I'm betting all my Hunters are feeling especially scared right now. We just learned that the Priestess is ruthless. I'm not proud of my namesake. We are protectors, not murderers. Little Anala is about to get an earful from the *real* Anala.

It's hard not to stand out when, as a group, we're dressed all in black in the middle of the day. A sunny (yes, another sunny day in England), warm July day. My Hunters are very thankful that July in England is much milder than July in California. At least, we wouldn't have to worry about dying from heat exhaustion today. However, getting anywhere without attracting unwanted attention might be a different story.

I can't wear my cloak. If I think my tight bodysuit would stand out, just imagine what the cloak would do. Especially in this area—the area of the Cloaked Priestess.

"Alright, I don't know how feasible this is, but let's not attract attention. We reach the cars and head to Abby's. They're obviously not using the cars we placed tracking devices on, which complicates things for us." Of course. "Sam will be driving the Jeep. We'll keep the same teams as last night. Whichever team is driving the Audi, stay behind Sam and follow his lead."

"I'll be driving," Jeremy announces, garnering looks that could kill from Amanda and Jenna. Jeremy is the quintessential alpha male. Or at least he was before he met me. I imagine his upbringing, being a quarterback and showcasing extreme machismo, has served him well. I don't recall him ever having trouble getting any girl he wanted. When I recruited him for the Society, I was worried I would have difficulty getting him to follow my lead. I feared he might be... well, like Malcolm, really. Maybe my knowledge and abilities changed his mind. Or perhaps having the other girls in the Society holding their own did. Whatever it was, I'm grateful. Though he does have his moments when the alpha male emerges. Leave it to Jenna and Amanda to bring him back down a notch if needed.

"Fine," I agree before any arguments could start. We don't have time for that. "Just be sure to stay as far away from us as you can. We each have trackers, so we'll always stay connected. Is everyone on the same channel on the walkies?"

They all inspect their equipment and nod.

"Good. Keep in constant contact, especially if we get separated at any point. I don't know what we're facing, so we need to be as cautious as possible."

"Are you still...in tune with us?" Amanda asks me, talking about how drinking drops of their blood connects us mentally. I can communicate with my Hunters through thoughts if I try hard enough to project clearly. They can't reply, but as long as I can lead them to safety, that's enough.

"Yes. If we reach the Priestess, do *not* speak to her directly. Let me handle it."

"I believe that's the way it has to be anyway," Emily responds. "Based on what we can gather from the journals, Tania, and even what we heard this morning, she will only speak with those she considers worthy. You are our Leader. To her, you're the only one she would consider worthy."

"They're on the move. Black S-Class Mercedes," Sam rattles off the license plate number to those in the SUV behind us. "Three occupants besides our targets. Driver and bodyguard in front, both male. Female passenger in back."

I smile at the authority in Sam's voice. I've never been known to go for men who challenge my own control and authority. Maybe that's why I'd never fallen in love before Sam. I feel a gentle squeeze of my hand, and I give Sam a little wink.

"Roger," Jeremy answers. "We have you in our sight. Jenna is looking over the map to see if any streets run parallel. If we can follow that way for a distance, hopefully they won't be suspicious."

"Good plan," I tell Jeremy, pride swelling in my chest. I made the right choice when I picked my Hunters. I could have searched more deeply for other Hunters to train. Older Hunters. But I decided to take a chance on those I knew, or semi-knew, as with Jenna, Jeremy, and the twins. I'm so glad I did.

CHAPTER FOURTEEN

"YOU ARE AN ELDER."

M y village isn't very big, but the mountains and valleys leave countless places to hide. I try to imagine myself as the 'new' Anala. Where would I go if I wanted to hide from the world but still maintain a sense of complete and total dominance?

"A mountain?" Sam asks softly.

"How terroristic," I reply snidely. I can't imagine doing that myself, but I see no fault in Sam's theory. It sounds like something a 'Priestess' would do. I pull out one of the journals I stole from Malcolm and flip through the pages, reading quickly. The one thing I notice clearly in each journal I read—those allegedly written by all of the 'Anala's,' as well as Emma—is their self-importance. Arrogance runs deep in these descendants. I'm almost offended. Almost. Honestly, if it weren't for my own arrogance, I wouldn't be here.

"Or with me," Sam reminds me gently. "Perhaps this was your destiny and not arrogance."

"Do you believe that? That we were destined to meet?"

"Don't you?" Sam replies, knowing the answer. "Your 'arrogance,' as you call it, wasn't about being able to rule everything, but these women? This arrogance they show is that they believe they are better than everyone else."

"I thought that as well," I tell him with guilt.

"I don't believe that. You only thought you were good, maybe even the best Hunter. But even you knew you still had more to learn from your parents. More to learn about being a Leader. I fear this Priestess believes she knows everything there is to know, and anything that contradicts her is punishable by death."

"I think you're right," Emily chimes in from the backseat.

The twins are so incredibly quiet that I sometimes forget they are there. Of course, I can sense them. Their scent is all around, but when I focus on Sam, it seems other things tend to fade into the background. I really should work on that.

"From what we've read," Emily continues as we all wait for her to elaborate, "there have been many deaths ordered by the Priestess because they've chosen not to follow her ways. It started with Emma. Those who did not agree with her vision of how things should progress didn't make it far enough to warn others."

"I can't believe that's what Emma turned out to be. She was so sweet when I knew her."

"Perhaps losing you and her brother is what changed her," Eric suggests.

I can see how that could happen when she lost Thomas. They were close. But me? How could I have not known that Emma looked up to me? So much so that she is keeping me 'alive' by giving my name to her own daughter, to be passed down for generations.

"That would mean she lost her humanity as a human," I say quietly, almost to myself. "I lost my parents. The only ones I had in my whole world, and I am Cursed. Yet, I held on to my humanity. How is it so easy for some to lose their compassion?"

No one says anything. I doubt they know what to say. We stay quiet as we follow the black sedan through familiar rolling hills. When they turn onto a narrow dirt road, we pass by at our usual speed so as not to draw attention.

"They turned onto a dirt road on the left," I tell Amanda and the others. They're far enough behind us that the twins can't see them, and they can't see us, but Sam and I know exactly where they are. "It's the only turn off on this road. Wait for a couple of minutes, then turn down it. Sam is going to drive a little further up and then turn around. Do not approach anyone until I get there."

"Got it," Amanda answers.

"If you see anyone..."

"Stop and hide," Jenna finishes. "I think we..."

"Wait!" I shout. "Don't go down the road at all!" Sam gives me a look, as do the twins. I can hear the others begin to protest, but I stop them. "Something doesn't feel right to me, guys. Pass the road, meet us."

"But, Ana..."

"Amanda, do as Anala says. Please," Sam pleads as he keys his mic on to enter the conversation. "You know her instincts are always spot on. If she is worried, *I'm* worried."

Part of me gets annoyed that Amanda agrees with Sam, but the less arrogant side - the one I'm working on - is thankful for the help.

"Stop right up here," I direct Sam.

"What are you feeling?" he asks as he complies.

"I don't know yet. I just... having them go down that road without me or you felt like certain death."

"Jesus," Sam mutters.

I don't know if I'm feeling this way because we just talked about how ruthless the Priestess is, or if these feelings are purely instinct. Either way, I'm not about to put it to the test.

We're leaning against the car as the others drive up and pull over. I can feel a presence around us but keep my thoughts to myself for now while I figure out how to handle the situation. I don't think Sam detects others nearby, and I wonder why that is. But before I get a chance to think more about it, Amanda and the others walk up to us, full of questions.

"What's going on?"

I frown. Not at Amanda, but at the presence. It's getting closer, and it's not alone.

"Ana?"

I don't mean to ignore Amanda, or anyone else that's trying to get my attention, but...

I walk to the edge of the road, gazing into the surrounding trees and meadow.

I know you're there, I say to the emptiness before me. I don't raise my voice because I know our company can hear me just fine. "Show yourself."

"Who are you?"

The voice is male. Rough enough that I can tell— even without their scent—that I'm dealing with Cursed Ones. I quickly look at my Hunters, noticing their confusion. All except Sam. The voice isn't perceptible to anyone who isn't Cursed.

Do not speak my true name. We don't know who these Cursed Ones are or if they work for the Priestess. Stay vigilant.

I see Sam give a slight nod and turn to the others, who huddle together as he whispers to them.

"Come out," I say aloud.

"You are Cursed. Are you one of Anala's?"

The question almost makes me laugh as much as it makes me cringe.

"No."

"Then why are you here?" the voice asks, and even with the roughness, I hear the curiosity.

"If you want to speak with me, show yourself," I demand.

I hear a distinct pause, followed by rustling leaves, before he emerges from the trees. My first thought is how impeccably dressed he is. It strikes me as very strange in this setting, and I can't help but wonder why he's hiding in the woods wearing a three-piece suit.

"I am here. Now it is your turn," he rasps.

"All of you," I answer.

He stares at me for a moment before raising his hand. With a flick of his wrist, the others with him reveal themselves. I quickly count and compare them to the different scents I can detect. Shaking my head, I raise an eyebrow and cross my arms, waiting.

"You are an Elder," he whispers, his eyes wide with surprise. "Come out."

Finally, his entire group stands before us. They keep their distance, cautiously watching my Hunters. Are they really that scared of us? What exactly is this Priestess doing?

"We have done as you asked," he announces, breaking me out of my inner thoughts. "Now it is your turn."

"What did you mean by Elder?" I ask, ignoring his request. Of course, being called an elder is not something I particularly enjoy, but his surprise at discovering that I am one piques my curiosity.

"You are not new, like him," he replies, gesturing to Sam with an irritated flick of his wrist. His blatant indifference toward Sam immediately makes me bristle.

"Careful," I warn. "How old are you?"

He hesitates. I wonder if it's because of the clear warning my voice carries, or because he's contemplating what to tell me.

"I have been this way for four hundred and fifty years. I am the eldest. The rest of my group ranges from one to three centuries. We are all that's left of the Elders."

"You are it?" I'm surprised. I don't know why, because in actuality, I thought I was the last to survive. But after finding out what is going on over here, I didn't anticipate this.

"Yes. Anala has eradicated the rest of the Elders in hopes of building an army of Cursed Ones she can control. She has turned Hybrids and Full Bloods against their Makers. She promises protection from the Hunters if they follow her."

How the hell can she turn the Cursed against their Makers? My bond with Sam is so strong that I can't imagine him turning against me. Of course, I know our situation is different, but even the thought of him...

Never going to happen.

Sam's words in my head are like balm to my soul. And now, I feel like a mush ball. My lips quirk when Sam laughs softly but immediately become serious again as I regard the group in front of me.

"You obviously know this is where she resides. Surely, she has her... 'army' here. Why would you come here?"

He hesitates and frowns again. It's almost as if he doesn't want to answer me, but feels he must.

"We do not want to live like this anymore. We have tried to fit in with humans; we try to imitate them as you obviously have," he explains, and I instinctively know he means trying to lose the roughness of their voices. Perhaps even trying to find their humanity. "And not ... hunt them. We have found humans who are sensitive to our situation."

My eyes narrow. "Sensitive to your situation?"

"They feed us when needed," he states firmly, almost daring me to criticize him. I can't really do so. Though I don't feed from my Hunters, they do give me drops of their blood. I also fed from Sam even before I changed him.

"That doesn't answer why you're here now," I say, deliberately skirting over the human feeder issue.

"We are trying to find a way to eliminate this problem."

"You want to kill the Priestess?"

His lips thin and eyes narrow as he studies me and my Hunters. "You have yet to disclose who you are. I have been more than accommodating in answering your questions. I would be appreciative if you would return the favor." He sounds like a lawyer. I wonder briefly if that is the profession he has chosen in his life.

I realize I have no reason to trust anything this guy has said. For all I know, he could be working for the damn Priestess. I turn to look at my Hunters, seeing him and his group flinch in my peripheral vision. Their stances shift, as if they're preparing to fight.

"Calm down. We are not going to hurt you unless we have to," I reassure him.

"They are Hunters. It is their destiny to kill those like us," he reminds me. "Are we to trust that you won't use them against us as the Priestess does?"

"Look, I don't know who this Priestess is. You obviously know that I am Cursed, and they haven't hurt me. What more proof do you want?" In reality, it *is* our job to kill them, but the information we may be able to gain is much more critical at the moment.

That is, until I see one of his group—an average-sized bloke dressed in jeans and a t-shirt with a black vest—curl his lip as he looks at my Hunters. He is clenching and unclenching his hands at his sides.

"Tell your boy to stand down," I sneer. "If you make us defend ourselves, all bets are off," I tell the obvious leader.

He glances at the jeans-wearing guy with a serious look. I watch amused as the guy drops his tough expression and steps back. The man in the three-piece suit looks at me.

"My name is Liam Culver. I am from Exeter."

CHAPTER FIFTEEN

"I WAS A HUNTER."

L iam remains quiet after his introduction to see if I respond in kind.

"I am Ana," I respond, opting to give my real name. Or at least a variation of it. "*This* is my village. Or was."

"You are from here? The land of the Leaders of the Society of Hunters?" His voice held a hint of awe, making me wonder. "How did you survive with the Cloaked One? Not that imposter," he says, jerking his thumb in the general direction we think the Priestess is in. "But the *real* Cloaked One?"

I survived because I *am* the Cloaked One. Of course, I don't say that out loud. Instead, I shrug with what I hope is nonchalance. I can't incriminate myself if I ignore the question.

"Do you know of the Cloaked One?" Liam asks.

"Of course."

The Priestess is pretending to be the Cloaked One." Surprisingly, he sounds disgusted by that. Almost as if it was disrespectful towards the one who sin-gle-handedly eradicated all — or at least what I thought was all - Cursed Ones.

"You cannot tell me you're a fan of the cloak," I laugh.

"I'd rather find my fate with another Cursed One than with this power-hun-gry bitch."

My eyebrows raise at the venom in Liam's voice. "She had your Maker killed, didn't she?"

"Yes. She turned one of my... brothers. I am lucky that she did not turn my charge against me." His eyes slant to his left. So, Liam is the hot-head's Maker. "You are this one's Maker." It's not a question as he motions to Sam.

"I am."

He nods, shedding some of his aversion toward Sam. "I know you are an Elder, but you have yet to tell me how long you have roamed this earth."

I smile at his wording. At least he didn't ask 'how old are you'. "600 years, give or take," I answer. To my utter shock, they all kneel before me. "No! Please. Get up."

"You are our Elder. You clearly came to help us. We must show you our respect."

"You do not need to kneel to show me respect. I am not your leader. I did not come here to help you." I raise my hand to stop his protest. "I did not even know about this Priestess until a couple of days ago."

"How could you *not* know? She is the most notorious Hunter around here since the disappearance of the *true* Cloaked One."

"We are not from around here," Sam answers, speaking for the first time.

"You're American." Liam studies my group, then focuses on me again. "There are no Cursed Ones in the States?"

"I can't possibly know the answer to that question. However, from what I have ascertained, Cursed Ones are not the norm. Nor are Hunters. I trained these guys," I say, gesturing to my group.

"You trained them? Why would you do that?"

"Because I needed them." I don't offer him any other information, and I can tell that frustrates him.

"If you are not here to help us..."

"I did not say I *wouldn't* help you. I need to get in to see the Priestess. I need to assess the situation before I can decide on what to do."

"She will kill you if she doesn't feel she can control you," Liam warns.

"Well, she can try." I know my arrogance is showing, but I'm having trouble believing that this 'Priestess' is as powerful as they say.

"You should keep your charge away from her if you choose to confront the Priestess."

"Sam would never turn against me," I tell him without hesitation. I'm pretty sure the look on my face made it clear that I didn't want to hear any arguments on the subject, for Liam said nothing. "How far is she from here?"

"No more than a kilometer down the hill."

I nod. We can't just go all gung-ho in there without a plan. I look at Liam's group, contemplating. Thirty-three Cursed Ones. Not exactly a huge army, but I'm hoping that with their age and help, along with my Hunters, we may be able to pull this off.

"If you want our help, follow us." With that, I turn my back on Liam and his group and get into the driver's seat of the Jeep, motioning to my Hunters. "Let's go."

Ten minutes later, I pull into an area that looks like a field of beautifully colored wildflowers. There are no buildings around, and it seems strange to me that my village has not grown or prospered much during the centuries I've been gone. In fact, this particular area appears to have been intentionally kept untouched except for regular maintenance. The grass and wooden fence surrounding the area have been perfectly preserved.

Without a word to anyone, I leave the car's confinement, walk to the middle of the area, and kneel, placing my hand on the ground.

"*Mum, papa.*" The words barely escape my lips. No one, not even the Cursed Ones, can hear me. But Sam feels it. Feels me. And in return, I sense the sympathy and sadness radiating from him. He doesn't come to me, instinctively knowing I need this time alone.

"Wait."

I hear the harshness in Sam's voice as he orders the others, including Liam and his group, to stay back.

"She is paying respect to the Leaders," Liam states, eliciting gasps from my Hunters. Liam, of course, doesn't know the significance of this moment to me, but my Hunters—my family—do. "I do not understand why a Cursed One would do this."

"It's not for you to understand," Sam tells him menacingly. "Give her a moment."

Sigh. I should have known better than to come here with Liam in tow. But I was drawn here. I had no choice but to follow my instincts.

"I was a Hunter." I stand and turn toward the others, addressing Liam. "Before I became what I am now."

Liam ponders that, and I let him. I need to get a hold of my emotions. *Are you okay?*

I nod slightly to Sam. "Tell me something, Liam. What was your plan before we came upon you?"

"We were going to 'storm the castle' so to speak," he answers without hesitation.

"Just like that? No plan?"

"We feel like plans are a waste of time. The more we wait, the more elders we lose. Between the Priestess and the Enforcers, we're quickly losing our advantage of being a stronger species."

"The Enforcers are against the Priestess. Why not use them to your advantage?" Naturally, I would *never* enlist Malcolm's help. He would, most certainly, want something in return. And then there's the fact that I'm a woman, so he wouldn't help me anyway. But Liam...

"Malcolm is a moron," Liam rasps. "He is as power-hungry as the Priestess. He uses us just as much as *she* does."

"So, you're on your own." Liam nods. "Are all Hunters either on the Priestess' side or an Enforcer?"

"Yes, it seems to be the case, except for your group. At least in these areas."

I nod distractedly, pondering my options. "Are you willing to do as I ask if we decide to help you?"

"You are our el..."

"Yeah, yeah, I'm older."

Jenna snickers and mutters something about retirement and menopause. I choose to ignore her childishness, though secretly I thank her for bringing a little levity to me as I stand in the place where my parents died.

"Will you take direction from me without issues?" I ask again. "*All* of you."

"Yes. We want this to stop, Ana. We are willing to do what it takes to make that happen."

"Very well. This is what is going to happen."

"No way!" Sam paces, furious about my plan.

"Sam..."

"No! I will *not* agree to this, Ana!"

I inwardly wince at his agitation.

"I'm with Sam." Amanda paces along with her brother, hands on her hips. She stops every third step just to glare at me.

"I suppose everyone else is, as well?" I ask dryly. Great job at letting Liam see who's boss around here. Interestingly enough, he stands back and just watches.

"Do you really think we're just going to sit back and watch you go into the snake pit by yourself?" Jenna asks, popping her gum for good measure. I know she's doing it to get on my nerves. It's working.

"Can we all just calm down and talk about this?" Emily chimes in. "Surely Ana has more to this plan than just her walking in and trying to reason with the unreasonable."

I do believe Emily just chastised me in her timid Emily way.

I give all of them a bored expression. Their shenanigans should get on my nerves, but honestly, I am grateful that they have minds of their own and challenge me to be a better leader.

"I do." I grab Sam's arm as he paces by me. "Stop, baby. Just listen to my plan. If at the end of my explanation you feel the need to add something, I will listen. Deal?"

Sam's eyes bore into mine, checking if I'm telling the truth.

Do you think I would lie to you?

I believe you will do what you think is necessary to keep us safe.

"You are together?"

Liam's question interrupts our internal conversation. I slant him a look but ignore his question. I think calling Sam 'baby' is explanation enough.

"I need all of you to surround the perimeter. You know the Priestess will have Hunters and maybe even Full Bloods nearby to protect her hideout. I want you to blend in."

"You want us to pretend to be hers?" Jeremy asks.

"Only the women can do that," Liam interjects. "Male Hunters are not allowed."

"What about Cursed Ones?" I want to know if Sam is safe.

"Male Cursed Ones are used by her, yes," Liam confirms.

"Will Jeremy and Eric be seen as Enforcers?"

Liam nods. Damn. There's a war between the Enforcers and the Priestess, and here we are, walking into the middle of it to fight both sides. Part of me wants to turn around, go back home to the States, and live a long, peaceful life with Sam. Let them kill each other. But the Hunter in me won't let me do that, at least not with a clear conscience. Honestly, I almost don't care.

CHAPTER SIXTEEN

"I PROMISE."

"So, you want us to hang around the perimeter while you waltz in and have a little chit-chat with your namesake?"

You know, when Jenna puts it that way, it sounds so incredibly simple. And incredibly stupid.

"You'll never make it inside." Liam's matter-of-fact attitude only serves to annoy me.

"Believe me, I will."

"What is your real plan, Ana?" I notice the way Sam has to force himself to call me Ana. It's still strange to me that he finds it much easier to call me by my given name since he's been Cursed. There's still so much to learn about being a Maker. Especially his. And because I am his Maker, he knows me way too well. Shit. He's really not going to like this.

"I'm just going to waltz in and have a little 'chit-chat' like Jenna said. As *myself.*"

I pause and let that sink in for Sam and the others. Liam and his group won't have any idea what it means, but I can see the exact moment it clicks for Sam.

"Like *hell* you are!" he shouts, startling me. Okay, Sam and I have had our little quarrels. Come on, the guy staked me. But I have never seen him this angry at me. I gotta say, I don't like it. Not only do I not like him being pissed at me, I don't like being yelled at. I'm just not the type of girl to sit back and take it.

"You dare yell at me?" I challenge, my own anger rising inside. "I am not only your Leader, I am your Maker!" Cheap shot, I know, but right now, I don't care.

"Leader? Maker? *You* are my goddamn *life*, Anala!"

Gasps fill the air, including mine. Not to mention Liam and the gang. I don't know if they all reacted for the same reason, but I know mine is from the anguish in Sam's words.

Faintly, I hear the sliding of swords being released from their hilts. But I don't turn away from Sam. I can't.

"Nothing will happen to me."

"You can't possibly know that," he retorts, frowning.

I close the distance between us and place a hand on his cheek. "I do. I won't allow anything to happen to me. Sam, I finally have something to live for. Do you think I would do something to take that away?"

"You are. You're walking into the unknown."

"You have to trust me, just as I have to trust that you and the others have my back. Think about it, baby. What could possibly throw them off more than the real thing?"

Sam's eyes flutter shut as he lowers his head, his shoulders slumping in defeat. I don't want this. I don't want him to be defeated. I want him with me, supporting me.

I do support you, baby. Sam grasps my hand that's on his cheek and brings it to his lips. *I think I screwed up calling you Anala.*

I turn slowly to see Liam and his group in full-out Cursed mode. 'Hulked out,' as Jenna puts it. My Hunters surround Sam and me in protective stances, swords out.

"This is unnecessary," I tell Liam. "If I wanted to hurt you, you would already be dead."

"Are you who he says you are?" Liam growls. Apparently, being in Cursed mode takes away some of his control over his voice.

"I am. But that is not all." I signal to Amanda, who runs to grab something from the Jeep. She hands it to me, and within the circle of my Hunters, I unfurl my cloak and whip it around me. Liam's eyes widen as I bring up my hood to cover my face.

"*The Cloaked One*," Liam whispers.

"Yes."

"I'm not sure whether I want to kill you or worship you." To my surprise, Liam smiles.

"How about neither, since I'm not sure whether I want to kill you either." I don't smile. I really am torn. I'm a Hunter. It is my destiny to kill the likes of Liam. But he has found a way to coexist with humans without harming them. At least that is what he has told me. "However, if you prove yourself to me, prove your loyalty to me, I'm sure we can work something out."

Sara glances at me, but wisely keeps quiet.

"*If* I find out that you have lied to me about how you treat innocents," I continue. "I will have no choice. Do you understand?"

Liam bows his head, partly in submission and partly to show his understanding. The rest of his gang follows suit, and I realize I have gained thirty-three supporters.

"You are the true Cloaked One. This land belongs to you," Liam says as he spreads his arms. "All territories rightfully belong to you according to the rules the Priestess has established from her inception. Not this Priestess, but her ancestors," Liam explains.

"I do not want this land. This is no longer my home. But I also do not want it ruled. Not in this way." I touch Amanda's shoulder, and she retracts her sword as the others do the same. "This war that the Enforcers and the Priestess have against each other serves no other purpose than to destroy the true meaning of the Society."

"Are you not doing that yourself by choosing to let us live?"

It is a bold question from Liam, considering it's his life on the line.

"I am. Though if we are honest, my parents broke the rules long ago when they allowed me to live. I have also broken the rules by cursing the one I love." I pause, considering my words carefully. "The Society was created to protect the innocent. I have continued to do so, despite being who I am. I changed Sam to protect him. I was not saved for personal gain, and though part of the reason I saved Sam was for selfish reasons, it was not to harm anyone."

"I think what Anala is saying," Amanda speaks up for the first time, "is that there are always exceptions to every rule."

"Your Hunters are very smart," Liam states, giving Amanda an appreciative look. Interesting. And if I interpret Sam's low growl correctly, he's not happy about it.

Calm, baby. Amanda can take care of herself.

Sam gives me a little grunt, and I can't help but grin at him.

"Yes, they are. Which is exactly why they will do as I say and stay back while I go in."

As if in slow motion, my Hunters all turn to me with unhappy looks. I raise an eyebrow in challenge. I know they are not happy with me or my idea, but I have no doubt they will do as I ask. What I do doubt is whether they will stay back if they feel my life is in danger.

"Please, baby. Please reconsider this."

"Sam, we've been over this. You know this is the best way."

"I don't know that. We haven't exactly had the chance to sit down and discuss all possible options."

"We do not have time, my love." My endearment surprises us both. I've never been one for mushiness, but with Sam, well, nothing is off limits. "We don't know when Malcolm plans to attack. Tania may or may not know of those plans. If she does, we will know how to proceed with him. If she doesn't, the Priestess will kill her. As much as I dislike her, I can't allow that to happen. She is an innocent."

"I still don't like you going in by yourself."

"You will be with me, Sam. You will know if I am in trouble. I trust you to be there when I need you."

"Anala?"

I reluctantly pull away from Sam's arms and turn to Liam.

The others and I will keep watch over your Hunters. You have my word. We are older than the ones the Priestess has chosen. The only reason she has been able to kill us off is that she used our charges against us."

"I appreciate that. My Hunters are highly capable, with abilities surpassing my expectations. However, having numbers is always advantageous."

Amanda passes Liam, lightly brushing her hand over his bicep. "Thank you," she says softly before turning to me. "We'll be as close as we can be. You know we'll do our best not to hurt innocents, but Ana..."

"Do what you must do. If it is possible, let Liam and the Cursed Ones handle the innocents. I care less about their conscience than I do yours. No offense," I say, glancing at Liam.

"None taken."

"Amanda, I trust all of you. I am counting on you all to be here, unharmed, when I get back. That includes you, Jenna," I smirk, trying to lighten the mood.

"Yeah, well, we're counting on you, too. So don't go getting your old ass killed." And, for good measure, Jenna pops her gum.

"You are such a bitch," I chuckle.

"True. But you love me anyway," she winks.

"Eh. You are growing on me, I suppose." I address all of my Hunters then. "You all know what you are to do. Be alert. Watch each other's backs."

Emily strides towards me and throws her arms around me. "I know we have had our problems, but I want you to know I understand everything you've had to do. *I don't blame you*," she whispers.

I swallow the lump in my throat and thank her before gently pushing her away.

"This is not good-bye. Please be careful. I will do the same." I exhale a nervous breath. I'm more worried about them than myself. "Let's get this show on the road."

"There are guards around the perimeter," Liam starts as we park in the same spot where we met him. "There are ways around them, but it will take longer. It will be easier to go through them."

"Are they innocents? Hunters?"

"Some."

"Then I'll take the long way." I hold Liam's gaze. "Do not kill anyone if you do not have to. The only reason I will forgive that kind of kill is if you are protecting my Hunters. Understood?"

"Of course. Anala, we have spent centuries working on becoming compatible with humans. You have nothing to worry about with us."

I nod slightly before turning away. It's time for me to go, and I'm trying to find my motivation. I don't want to leave Sam. When I'm with him, I know he's safe. Now, both of us will be a little distracted, which could be deadly.

"Baby." I bring my arms up and around Sam's neck. "We have to concentrate on what is going on around us."

"I know," he murmurs, his face buried in my hair.

"Promise me you'll be here when I get back."

"I promise." He lifts my chin to stare at me intently. "Now it's your turn. Promise me you're going to come back to me."

"I promise."

CHAPTER SEVENTEEN

"HESITATION."

I follow the directions Liam gave me, again moving through the trees to stay undetected. I wish I had used my time with Tania to learn more about this 'Priestess'. Like, what does she look like? I'm sure I won't have trouble figuring out which one she is, of course. If her ego is as big as I think it is, she'll be sitting on a throne. I'm also sure she'll be wearing her damn cloak. Well, two can play that game. And, I made the cloak what it is centuries ago.

But how old is she? Will she resemble Emma? Or Thomas? Or maybe she'll look like Sam and Amanda. Damn. I didn't think of that. Will I be able to defeat her if I see Sam in her eyes? What I do know is that she is definitely a Hunter. She was born into the Society simply because she is a descendant of the Lagans. In fact, being part of that family means she is technically under my leadership. Not that I think she would accept that in any way whatsoever.

I leap to the last tree before the Priestess' small hideaway. It's not quite a cave, so it has been manmade. A dwelling built mostly underground, with just the entrance visible from what looks like a normal hill to onlookers. Two 'guards' stand in front of the door, and by their scent, they are Cursed. Good. That makes it easier for me since I have no shame in killing them.

I'm here, baby. Is everyone okay?

We're fine. We're doing what we can to blend in. It has been difficult for Jeremy and Eric, but we have it handled. Be careful, Anala.

Back at ya, babe. Going in.

Wait!

My heart races upon hearing Sam's plea, wondering what could have caused such panic in him.

Sam?

I love you, Anala. Remember your promise to me.

I let the tension in my shoulders relax a little, knowing no one has been hurt.

I love you, too, Sam. I remember.

I take a deep breath and descend quietly to the ground. I flip my cloak's sides back and draw my swords from their sheaths, pressing the buttons to extend the blades. I pause to consider my options. I need to reach the door as silently as possible. While my speed is an advantage, they are too far apart for me to incapacitate both with my swords at once. There's a risk of drawing attention if one manages to escape while I am distracted by the other. With my mind made up, I stab the tips of my swords into the ground and draw my daggers. Holding their blades in each hand, I give a quick flick of my wrists to strike precisely where I intend. They immediately drop to their knees, giving me the perfect opportunity. I grab my swords and rush toward the entrance.

Hesitation. It's never been a problem for me when it comes to killing Cursed Ones. So why is it now? I shake off the guilt I feel before bringing my swords down on the necks of the two felled vamps. I dust off my daggers that dropped to the ground when the two disintegrate, and sheathe them back on my thighs.

Doors are unlocked. Apparently, they're very confident in their abilities and the protection here.

Ego. It may just bite them in the ass.

I chuckle softly at Sam's thoughts, feeling more confident about my actions just hearing him. We say no more. We don't need to because it's already been said. We know to be cautious. We know we love each other. Now, it's time to buckle down and stay focused.

I open the door to a long, dark hallway. What's with these people? It's almost as if they're mocking the Society and Cursed Ones. Hunters were never like this back in my day. We didn't have old, gothic-style homes. Neither did the Cursed Ones. Hell, the cursed roamed the land like animals looking for prey. And here I am, again, in yet another medieval 'headquarters' straight out of some Hollywood horror movie. I haven't missed the irony that even in medieval times, when I was a kid, I didn't come across places like this.

I freeze, using all my senses to adapt to my surroundings and figure out my next move. The dark, of course, doesn't matter to me. I can see as clearly as if it were daytime. I'm just trying to decide which way to go and who I might be up against. All heat, scents, and activity seem to be coming from one spot. That tells me they've all gathered in one place. Either they're waiting for what Tania has to say, or they're there to witness her death.

I concentrate my hearing, but the walls are too thick to hear anything except the occasional murmur.

Sam? Were you able to get close?

Yes.

Sam's short answer, as well as the feelings he invoked in me, have me pausing.

What happened?

Don't worry about us. Just focus on what you need to do.

Sam. What happened?

Hesitation. I'm starting to dislike that word and how it makes me feel.

We did what we had to do.

Damn. Innocents have fallen. I can only hope that one of my Hunters wasn't the one who had to do it. I'm pretty sure I would be able to feel it if it was Sam. At least I hope so.

Is everyone okay?

Yes, baby. It wasn't one of us, but they had to watch. It wasn't pleasant, but it was necessary. We're at the entrance and will remain here unless you need us.

I shake off the sadness I feel knowing that this war—hell, this charade of having Rulers, territories, and fake Analas and fake Cloaked Ones—is killing humans. This is not what the Society is about. My anger only strengthens my resolve to end this madness. I follow the scents, staying close to the wall, my swords still at the ready. Soon, a light pierces the darkness, and I know I'm close when I hear voices clearly.

"Bring her in."

It's a woman's voice with a slight Irish lilt, and I instinctively know it belongs to the Priestess. I sniff the air, trying to distinguish her scent. It's familiar. Sam's scent is incredibly strong to me—enticing, really. This scent carries remnants of Sam's, similar to Amanda's, and I am certain that this Priestess is related. Fantastic. I almost press myself against the wall as I move closer to observe.

The first thing I notice about the Priestess is how much she resembles Sam and Amanda. She has the same wheat-colored hair and golden eyes. However, the difference is how cold her eyes are. There's no spark, no love. In fact, I realize then that the Priestess didn't remind me of Sam and Amanda at all. It was Thomas.

I automatically lean against the wall when I see them bring Tania in. My mood immediately worsens, but I hold it back—with great effort, of course—and listen in.

"Priestess. I'm honored that you . . . "

"I have not given you permission to speak," the Priestess says coldly, cutting off Tania. Tania immediately bows her head as the Priestess turns to Abby. "You brought her here. I trust you have a good reason."

Abby steps forward and clears her throat. "Yes, Priestess. She is Malcolm's sister and has heard his plans against you."

Tania visibly swallows and cowers when the Priestess turns her gaze back on her.

"Is this true?"

"Yes, Priestess."

Fake Anala says nothing at all, and I inwardly wince, almost hoping Tania will speak. Does she not realize that the Priestess is waiting for her?

"Well? Are you going to tell me?" The irritation in the Priestess's voice is enough to intimidate those around her. To me, it is simply annoying.

"I, um..."

I see Tania frown. Shit.

She can't remember.

I can sense Sam's confusion even before he asks.

What do you mean?

If Tania knew Malcolm's plans before, she doesn't remember them now. The Priestess is going to kill her, and it's my fault.

The guilt weighs on me like nothing I've ever experienced. I didn't intend for her to forget everything, just me and my Hunters. What have I done?

Baby, it's not your fault.

I barely hold back my scoff. Of course, it's my fault. But I don't have time to argue with Sam about it. For once, I have no idea what to do. After centuries of living, I finally find myself in a situation I don't know how to get out of.

Sam, if I don't go in there, they will kill Tania and her friends. If I do, I will have to kill... innocents.

They are all around—hunters, innocents, humans—surrounding this Priestess as if she were some larger-than-life creature. They would lay their lives down for her. And, though I know my Hunters would do the same, this person doesn't deserve it. How do I hold on to my humanity if I have to kill...

We're on our way. Please wait until we arrive before doing anything. Anala? Please.

Hurry.

I stand my ground, hoping that Tania can come up with something to save her ass.

"You dare come here and make a fool of me!" the Priestess bellows. She whips around and points a finger at Abby. "You! You said she knew something! You told me she is Malcolm's sister. You dare to ask for an audience with me and have *nothing*!"

Even I flinch at the deafening scream the Priestess lets out. My Hunters choose that moment to walk up behind me, and I raise my hand to halt their advance.

"I have no use for incompetent followers. You were in that house with him, were you not?" She waits for Tania to nod in agreement, then continues. "You should know his plans. How worthless you are."

My blood begins to boil. I dislike Tania a lot, but this is not how a leader should speak! I turn to the others, pointing at Liam and his gang and gesturing for them to come closer. Taking a deep breath, I project my thoughts to all of my Hunters.

Stay here. I raise my hand again before they can even think to argue. *I do not know what is going to happen in there. I want you out here in case all hell breaks loose. There are roughly eighty humans in there and another ten Cursed Ones. Do you understand what I am saying? I cannot risk you killing an innocent. Guard the door. Do not let anyone pass. I am going to do everything I can to diffuse the situation.*

Reluctantly, they nod, but I can see Sam fuming. I focus my thoughts entirely on him.

Please trust in me.

Sam moves closer and gives me a gentle kiss on the lips.

I do.

Chapter Eighteen

"She isn't me."

I glance at Liam, and he nods in understanding. I hope he truly understands that what I want to do is incapacitate if necessary, but not kill. The only reason I'm taking them instead of my group is in case things escalate. I hear the Priestess order Tania, Abby, and Monica to kneel before her. I try to tune out the rest because, honestly, I don't want to hear her biting remarks.

"You three are sentenced to death. The Society does not need useless..."

"Enough!" I step through the archway in full Hunter gear, hood up, hiding my face. My voice is disguised—harsh and threatening. The Priestess's head snaps up quickly, surprise clear on her face, along with outright fury at being interrupted, I assume.

There is hesitation among the others in the room. Hands are on their swords, which, as far as I can tell, range from katanas to broadswords.

"What are you waiting for!" the Priestess yells. "Get them!"

"I would not do that if I were you," I say menacingly, putting intense power into my voice as Liam and his group file in behind me. There is a lot of confusion in the room. I don't think anyone was expecting another Cloaked One. Especially one as commanding as I am. Is that my arrogance? Maybe. But I prefer to think of it as confidence.

"Wh - who are you?" For the first time, the Priestess's own confidence falters.

I ignore her and deliberately walk through the stunned crowd, closing in on Tania and her friends. Of course, all my senses are heightened, and I feel Sam's apprehension as if it were my own. I'm essentially turning my back on Hunters trained to kill me. But that doesn't mean I don't know exactly where they are, and even more, where their swords are. Once I reach Tania, I lightly touch her shoulder. She looks at me, then at the Priestess, then back at me. Confusion is clear in her eyes.

"Stand."

Now, I don't think my 'namesake' has fully recovered from her initial shock as she watches, dumbfounded, while Tania rises. I consider releasing Tania from my compulsion, but she will remember Sam and the others then. Right now, they are my ace in the hole. I can't risk Tania exposing them at this moment. I glance at Abby and Monica, who are still kneeling but are staring at me as if they have entirely forgotten their Priestess.

"Stand," I command them, and they comply. I then raise my eyes to my namesake. "You have made a mockery of the Society. *This*," I spread my arms wide, encompassing the entire room, "is *not* what the Society was created to do."

"I don't know who you think you are, but this is *my* Society. I rule here. *I* rule *everywhere*! It is my birthright."

"Your birthright?" I scoff. "You were about to *murder* innocents! Who told you that was acceptable in the Society?"

"I am the Society! I make the rules just as my ancestors did before me. I will do as I see fit! I will not allow my Society to be flooded with incompetent Hunters! My mother, grandmother, and those before them have done the same for longer than you have been alive. Do not think you can come in here and tell me how to run my Society!"

I was patient. Believe me, it was difficult, but I let her finish her little tirade before laughing at her. The bright red flush that covered her furious face was nearly comical.

"That is exactly why you are not fit to be the Leader," I castigate. "It is not about *you*. It is about the greater good of innocents and your Hunters."

To my surprise, she then laughs at me. "Are you that naïve?"

"No. I am just not *that* arrogant to think everyone should bow to me."

"Bow to you?! You are nothing! An imposter! You come in here wearing that fake cloak and think you can stand up to me?" This Anala was infuriated. Her face flushing with anger, her words sputtered with barely contained violence.

"Oh, sweetie. It is not I who is the imposter," I say, my voice saccharine sweet, pissing her off even more. Slowly, I lift my hands and remove my hood from my face. "It is you."

I am in full Cursed mode, having made the change during the Priestess's little ego speech. The sight has the desired effect on little Anala, as she steps back with an audible gasp.

"Anala?"

The rough female voice startles me, as it didn't come from anyone nearby. My head snaps up - as does the Priestess's - landing on Cursed eyes and very familiar features.

"Mother?"

Mother? Mentally, I recall the young girl I almost killed when she followed Thomas and me on patrol. I add a few years to that face, and now it's my turn to be shocked.

"Emma?" No. It can't be. Can it?

"You are dead. Thomas told me. How is this possible?"

Emma is as confused and amazed as I am, I think. I was astonished—and dismayed—when I found out that Thomas was still...alive. Now, knowing Emma is as well? Had Thomas known? Disappointment fills me to see that she is as power-hungry as her brother was.

"The same way you are still here, I'm guessing," I respond dryly. "Why are you still here, Emma? What made you do this to yourself?"

"Did you really think I would trust anyone else to train my descendants? I had to be here to ensure the right daughter was chosen to take over each time. I won't let my vision be compromised by anyone who doesn't understand."

"And she is the one you chose?" I snap, angrily gesturing to the Priestess.

"Mother? What is happening? How can you let this subordinate speak to you like that? Why are you not ordering the death of this...person?" Little Anala is beyond annoyed that I am still breathing, apparently.

115

"Hush, child," Emma chastises, still looking at me. I wonder if she's trying to figure out if I really am who she remembers from centuries ago.

"What is happening here, Emma? This is not what my parents envisioned for the Society."

Anger distorts Emma's still young face. "You were not there after your parents died. You have no idea what we went through. I took charge!"

"Took charge?! You ruined the Society!" My namesake snarls and steps toward me. "If you want your Anala to live, order her to back off!"

Emma laughs at me. "I trained her to fight like you, Anala. Do you think she's afraid of you?"

"Do I think she is? No, probably not, because her arrogance and yours will not allow her to be. Do I think she should be? Oh yes." I turn my glare to the younger Anala but still address Emma. "You may have trained her to be like me, but there's one problem. She isn't me."

My problem now is this: Anala is innocent. I don't want to kill her. Emma, on the other hand... Fast as lightning, I end up behind Emma with a stake aimed at her heart. Young Anala stammers pleas to let 'Mother' go.

"Why have you done this, Emma?" I ask, my mouth close to her ear.

"After you died, Thomas went a little crazy," she begins with a touch of uncertainty. "You were supposed to marry him, have children, and continue the Society as the Leaders."

"My father would never have agreed to that," I interrupt. I still can't believe this whole "betrothed" thing with Thomas. My parents knew that wasn't what I wanted. All I wanted was to be the best Hunter. I am smart enough to admit I had feelings for Thomas. I will even say I was infatuated with him. But I would never have agreed to marry Thomas. And this story about us taking the place of my parents as the Leaders of the Society? Something about that just doesn't seem right to me. My parents weren't even close to retiring and handing the reins over to me.

"*My* father told me it was the reason we moved from Ireland - to be close to your family."

Then he did it of his own accord, I think scathingly.

116

"But we lost you and then Thomas. Not to mention losing your parents as well. We needed leaders. My parents stepped up, but no one would be as loyal to them as they were to your parents. And you."

That bit of information shocks me, but I take it with a grain of salt. I can't be sure if Emma is telling me the truth, the truth as *she* knows it, or just bullshit to get me to see things her way.

"I was a kid, Emma. No one was afraid of me."

"Are you kidding? Anala, you were the talk of the Society. Everyone knew you would be the Leader soon. It was inevitable because of who your parents were, but it was more than that. They feared you. Your skill, your composure, your complete control. That is why I chose to name my daughter Anala and ensured the tradition was carried on. I trained them to be as you were. Hunters aren't even afraid of Cursed Ones, but they were afraid of you. And they would be afraid of my daughters."

My grip tightens on her. "That is not what the Society is about. We are not supposed to reveal ourselves to innocents, and we must support each other. Being a leader isn't about making people fear you. It's about earning their loyalty because they know you're loyal to them.

"That is outdated. To lead, you need a ruler who commands fear. They must understand who is in charge, or chaos will follow. And this land is ours. It belongs to my daughters and me. Anyone seeking peace must prove they are deserving. Join us. With the true Anala, we will be unstoppable."

Emma's voice shifted when she said those words. Before, she spoke with indifference, authority, and entitlement. Asking me to join her transformed her voice to one of reverence.

"This land is not yours," I tell her roughly. "It belongs to me. And you have not proven your worthiness to me..."

Baby.

My eyes, which had lost focus, take a moment to recognize Sam's presence. Not only in my mind but also at the back of the room where he holds my gaze. Confusion settles within me, and I realize I'm afraid of the feelings I had when speaking of this land that belongs to me. Arrogance. Entitlement. Authority. All of which I heard from Emma. If it hadn't been for Sam's silent interference...

I'm okay now.

Sam nods slightly, with a small smile. He is my calm. My grounding. Perhaps at this moment, my humanity.

"I am beginning to think your family had issues," I tell Emma. "You were all power hungry. Thomas believed that he could take over mankind by building an army of Cursed Ones."

Emma gasps. My namesake screams at me about being a liar, telling 'Mother' not to listen to me.

"Thomas died," Emma rasps.

"He offered himself up for the change, Emma." I say this without trying to soften the truth for her. She needs to understand the reality. She's just as ruthless as Thomas was. "He was merciless. He killed innocents without hesitation. He was a Hunter, Emma, just as you were meant to be, and he didn't let that stop him." I push the stake closer, the point denting the fabric beneath it with the pressure. "He murdered my parents."

"You are lying."

"You know I'm not." From my peripheral vision, I see little Anala reach for her sword. I don't know what she's planning, since there's no way she can get to me before I kill Emma. Then I see her glance at Tania, and I understand. Damn. Tania has too much information for me to let her be killed. And yes, I admit I hesitate when it comes to saving her life.

CHAPTER NINETEEN
"CHEAP SHOT."

S tay alert. Things are about to get crazy.

I make sure I project my thoughts to all of my Hunters, and I hear them take a collective breath. All I can do now is ask whatever entity is listening to keep them safe.

All of this happens in just a few seconds. Little Anala reaches for her other sword, and I find it ironic that having that second sword actually gives me an advantage over her. She should have been trained to go for both of them simultaneously, I think as I push the stake fully into Emma and sprint toward my namesake. It takes me less than a second to reach her, a little longer than that for her to realize what I've done, and just another instant for her to turn her swords on me with an incredibly impressive war cry.

My swords are out and ready, and I lift them just in time to deflect the slicing motion rushing toward my neck. I raise my leg, and with only a small portion of my strength - not enough to kill her or break all her bones — I kick her across the room. Our swords spark as they slide against each other, and she crashes into the other Hunters and Cursed Ones in her path. They fall like bowling pins. Bowling pins with confused faces.

Remember. Incapacitate. There are far too many innocents in this room. We need to be careful. Sam, I'm pretty sure Liam understands, but make sure.

I will.

Whatever you do, keep Tania alive. We need her.

Shock and amusement flood my mind, and I recognize those are the feelings my Hunters are experiencing. I should have obtained Malcolm's plans from Tania earlier. Unfortunately, I was too damn distracted. I keep reminding myself that she's human. An innocent. I must protect her.

Purposefully, I stalk toward young Anala. Swords slash at me, some with determination, others half-heartedly. But I don't let any of them slow me down.

"You killed her!" the 'Priestess' yells, anger filling her voice and actions as she charges at me. It makes me wonder when Emma trained her, did she teach her that anger weakens your control.

"You are a terrible Hunter if you believe that," I mock, arcing my arm, causing her blade to ricochet off mine. Unfortunately, blocking her means I miss another sword coming at me from behind. The Katana slices through my bicep down to the bone. I'm pretty sure the only thing saving my arm from being completely cut off is the heaviness of my cloak. Good thing I have it on, because even I can't grow back an appendage. Blood pours out before the cut heals rapidly. Son of a bitch, that hurts! The Katana strikes again, this time aiming higher, and I do a backflip to keep it from chopping my head off. The next thing I know, Sam is there, fending off the Michonne wannabe. Thank God.

My grip on my sword slips because of the blood running down my arm, making that hand pretty useless. Fantastic. It's not like I can just put it down to wash my hands. I press the button to retract the blade of the sword in my right hand—the one covered with blood—and slide it into its sheath at my hip. Thank goodness I'm ambidextrous, since I can't hold much of anything until I can wipe my hand off.

"Why did you come here! You don't belong!" The Priestess keeps slashing haphazardly. Seriously? Is this really how she was trained, or is she letting her emotions guide her? Like when Emily attacked me after I killed Zac, it makes her movements erratic and unpredictable. But it also leaves her open to serious damage if I choose to land a strike.

"If you hadn't screwed up so monumentally, I wouldn't have to be here," I taunt. I know it's going to make her even more volatile. I'm just hoping I can use it to my advantage.

"*I* am what these people need! They are followers! Mother chose me over my sister because I was stronger!"

"Where is your sister now?" I ask, swinging my blade in what has become a duel between just the two of us. I wonder if this is what she demands of her 'disciples'. By letting her fight her own battles, it only proves her formidability. Unless, of course, it becomes too much for her, I assume, since she is beginning to look panicked and out of her depth. Honestly, she's a disappointment to me.

"It doesn't matter where she is," she scathes and swings again. "All that matters is *I* am here, and these people bow to *me*!"

I see a couple of heads turn our way with looks of contempt. She may think she has devotees, but I sense a desire for mutiny. Point for me.

"You killed her, didn't you?" I don't know how I know that, but I do. It makes a little more sense to me now that this Anala isn't exactly ranked in the top ten 'Great Hunters'.

"You don't know anything!" She swings her sword at me, and I swing back, causing her to twirl with the force of my blow. Just as I'm about to press forward and end this little duel between us, I hear Sam grunt in pain. At the same time, I feel a sharp pain in my right side. The pain is enough to make my knees buckle, and I glance behind me to check if Sam is okay.

Baby?

I'm good. Cheap shot.

Geez. I shake my head. He's such a man. God forbid he ever admits to letting his guard down.

"Baby, look out!"

Fear brightens Sam's eyes, and I turn just in time to see my namesake's sword heading straight for my neck. Oh, the irony. There isn't enough time for me to dodge the oncoming sword, so I lean backward as quickly and as far as I can, hoping it's enough to keep my head. I feel the sharp edge of the blade cutting through my neck, slicing from one side to the other, deep enough for me to doubt I will be able to heal from this.

"Anala! No!"

Dimly, I hear Sam's cries, but before I can respond, my knees buckle. I feel myself falling.

Through blurred vision, I see the Priestess coming after me to finish the job, and Sam raises his sword. Murder is in his eyes and thoughts, and though I can barely lift my arm, I try to get his attention.

"*Baby, no*," I whisper, my voice gurgling from the blood. I have no idea how deeply I'm cut, but I can tell that I'm not healing. At least not fast enough to stop the pain.

Before the words leave my mouth, a blur of motion rushes past us, and the Priestess is soaring through the air, a fully Cursed Liam wrapped around her. I vaguely notice the pointed end of her sword protruding from his back.

"Ana!" Amanda screams as she, Jenna, and Emily drop to their knees beside me and Sam, while Jeremy, Eric, and Sara surround me, fending off any potential attackers. "Oh God, oh God, oh God! She's not healing! Sam! She's not healing!"

"I know!" Sam's voice is gruff, full of anguish. "Baby, why aren't you healing? What's happening?"

"*I don't know*." It hurts to talk, and even when the words come out, they're barely a whisper.

I can't speak, Sam. It hurts.

What can I do? Tell me what to do, baby, please!

I don't know what it feels like to faint. I don't think I've ever fainted in my six hundred years of living. Even when I was human, I never blacked out. But I'm pretty sure what I'm feeling now means I'm close to passing out.

Liam ambles up beside us, unceremoniously pulling out the Priestess's sword from his stomach. "How is she?"

"She's not healing," Amanda replies. Different thoughts race through my mind at this moment. One is what happened to my namesake, and another is wondering if Amanda is in shock and stuck on repeat.

I barely hear Liam ordering his group to circle us and ensure no one reaches me.

"Baby, please. I need you. Tell me what to do." Sam's fear is breaking my heart. He has my head cradled in one hand while the other tries to staunch the flow of blood spilling out of me. I just don't know what to tell him or how to fix this. I've never been this hurt before. I've never not healed immediately. I can only think of one thing, and it's not something I want to do.

I'm already in Cursed mode; I have been since I walked into that room. Since that hasn't helped me heal faster, maybe feeding will.

I need blood, Sam.

Take it from me. He responds immediately. *Take all that you need, baby.*

Sam leans closer to me, exposing his neck. Damn it. I never wanted anyone to see me do this, especially my Hunters. Most specifically, Amanda. Knowing that I do this, that this is who I am, is one thing, but actually seeing it is altogether different. But I don't think I have any other choice.

I glance at Amanda. *"I'm sorry,"* I whisper before closing my eyes, closing everyone out, and sinking my teeth into Sam. The gouge in my throat doesn't make this very easy.

Bite your wrist, Sam. Drip some of the blood into the cut. I command as I drink heavily from him.

Without taking his neck from me, Sam complies, swiftly biting into his wrist and placing it over my throat. The blood - what I'm drinking and what Sam is giving me from his wrist - is like a miracle ointment. A wound that would have killed a human almost instantly is disappearing, closing up as though it were being sewn by an invisible thread. I feel my body begin to regain its strength, as well as the other side effects that happen when I drink from Sam.

Enough, baby. That's enough. I retract my teeth from Sam, gently pushing him away. His breathing is as erratic as mine, his pupils dilated. *I know it's difficult, but we must control it.*

"Ana?"

I jump when Amanda's hand touches my blood-soaked shoulder. Wrenching my eyes away from Sam, I focus on her.

"I'm fine. Better. I'm sorry, Amanda," I tell her again remorsefully. Oh, what I would have given for her not to have seen me drinking from her brother.

"Don't be. We understand. *I* understand. It's okay."

"What happened? How did she get the drop on you?"

"It was my fault." It's Sam who answers Jenna, his voice still husky from my feeding on him.

"No, Sam."

"It was. You were distracted because I allowed myself to get cut. If it weren't for me..."

"Stop! Sam, that's enough." Getting into a sitting position, I take Sam's face in my hands. "It happened in the heat of battle. We may have both let our guard down for a moment out of fear for each other, but it doesn't matter now. I'm still here because of you. You are not to blame." Sam lowers his eyes. I lift his chin until he's looking me in the eye. "I love you. I had to make sure you were okay. It was *my* mistake not to keep an eye on her. Not yours. You were only trying to protect me from Katana girl. Please, baby."

He nods and leans in to kiss me softly. Sigh. I definitely don't need that in my state. I want it, but I don't want to fight that along with everything else right now.

We can't do this, Sam. You know I want more.

I know. I love you, too, by the way.

We smile at each other before standing. I shake off the lingering effects of losing a lot of blood in just a few minutes. It takes me a moment to realize that all activity has stopped around us.

"What did you do to her?" I ask Liam.

"What I had to do," he responds nonchalantly.

"You killed her?" I try to curb my anger as I stare him down.

"She nearly killed you. Damn, she almost killed me. What did you expect me to do?"

"Incapacitate, Liam!"

"I tried, Anala." Liam lost a bit of his aloofness and even looks somewhat sheepish. "I did not mean to kill her, I swear. She just kept coming at me. I know you know how much it hurts to be stabbed. I tried stopping her. My strength and anger got the best of me. I apologize."

"Ana. We can't save everyone." My gaze turns to Amanda, who is apparently siding with Liam. "I mean, she was crazy. I believe Liam when he says he didn't have a choice."

"Oh, good. You agree with killing innocents."

"Sarcasm is my thing, Ana," Jenna scoffs. "Of course, we don't agree with killing innocents. However, when it comes to us or them, we are trained to protect ourselves and one another. *You* trained us that way. And Liam has pledged his allegiance to you."

"Exactly," Amanda continues. "If it weren't for Liam, Sam would have killed the Priestess. You *know* he would have. Liam did you a favor. In more ways than one."

"Alright. Fine, I get it." My attention returns to Liam. "Thank you. I should have said that first, and because I didn't, I apologize."

"I understand."

It is eerily quiet in a room that just moments ago was filled with chaos.

"Why did they stop fighting?"

"Because their Priestess is dead." Liam points to young Anala's body, suspended from the sword that Liam had thrust through her and into the wall behind her.

CHAPTER TWENTY
"WELL, DUH."

"Jesus! Take her down!" Turning my back on the sight, I address my Hunters as Liam acquiesces, motioning for a couple from his group to help. "Are you all alright?"

"Yes." Jeremy steps up to me and surprises me with a hearty hug. "Thought we lost you there for a minute, A. Don't do that again."

I chuckle softly. "I'll try not to, since it hurts like a son of a bitch." My eyes scan over each of them, making sure there are no serious injuries. A few cuts and bruises here and there, but nothing too bad. At least none of them were bitten. I honestly don't think I could have gone through that again.

"What do we do now?" Sara has picked up a discarded piece of clothing from nearby and is trying to wipe some of the blood off me. It's actually a kind gesture I wouldn't have expected from her.

"I need to release Tania and get some information from her." I stop Sara's ministrations when she refuses to look me in the eye. "She is still alive, right?"

"Yes. She is sitting next to Emma, along with her friends."

"Is there something you want to say?"

"Do you think releasing her is a good idea? What if she..." Sara pauses, glancing at Sam. "Are you in the right frame of mind not to kill her if she says or does something stupid?"

A valid—very valid—concern. Especially given my current state from drinking from Sam. But I need the information Tania has about Malcolm's plans. If he decides to drop by today, we won't be ready. My Hunters are exhausted.

I look Sara straight in the eye and answer, "You are here to help keep me grounded. All of you are. I trust you to help me if I need it."

Sara seems to think about my answer for a moment then nods. Before I get a chance to talk more with my group, Liam approaches me, holding the lifeless body of the Priestess.

"What would you like me to do with her, Anala?"

My eyes flutter closed briefly as I say a small prayer for her loss, as well as for the others who have fallen. I don't know the full extent of the damage yet, or if my Hunters caused it. That will have to wait. Great. Something to look forward to.

"Put her next to her... 'Mother'," I answer softly.

Are you okay?

I squeeze Sam's hand when he slips his into mine. It's not an answer, but it's the only one I have right now.

"What will you do with Emma?"

I contemplate Amanda's question for a moment. I don't believe there are any other alternatives. Emma will have to meet the same fate her brother did—death by my hand.

"She will be with Thomas again."

It's bad when just the sight of a person makes your blood boil. Jealousy is a peculiar emotion. I know Sam would never betray me, yet knowing Tania wants him still pisses me off. Taking a deep breath, I roll my shoulders to try to ease some of the tension there. It's time to release Tania. Yippie.

"Rise, Tania," I command. She obeys and stands before me. Her eyes are still glazed over from my compulsion. Abby and Monica watch me, their faces showing mixed emotions. Wariness and interest create an amusing expression. And, yes, I am stalling. "Tania, you are released from my compulsion."

She blinks rapidly, then looks at me wide-eyed. Her eyes dart from side to side as I'm sure she's remembering everything that had happened to her. Abruptly, she staggers back away from me, pointing accusingly.

"You! You're Cursed!"

"Well, duh."

That brilliance comes from Jenna. Couldn't you guess?

"Yes. I think we've all well established that I am Cursed, Tania. Now, I need information from you."

"The Priestess will kill you!"

"You mean *that* Priestess?" I ask, pointing to the prone body. It hurts to be so flippant about a life lost, but I swallow the self-deprecation and focus.

"*No.*"

Astonishingly, Tania appears devastated by the loss of someone who, not even thirty minutes ago, wanted to kill her.

"You're a murderer! Just like Malcolm!"

"I didn't kill her." It's futile to try to explain that to her in her state, so I don't elaborate. "However, Malcolm is just the person I want to talk about."

Tania tears her eyes away from the body and glares at me. She then glances at Sam, and I see something flicker in her eyes. I clench my fists at my thighs, willing myself to keep them there and not strangle the life out of her.

"So, you still need something from me?" She smiles smugly, then sends Sam what I'm guessing is supposed to be an alluring look. "I still need something from you."

Sam grabs me and holds me tight as my Hunters stand in front of me. They're not paying attention to Tania but are all focused on me.

"Ana, don't let her get to you," Amanda pleads. "She knows how to push your buttons. She's just too stupid to know what a mistake that is. Come on now, we have a job to do."

"Ma'am?"

Okay, even though I'm furious, the timid call of 'ma'am' still amuses me enough to wonder who they're talking to. I look around my group and see Abby speaking to...me. Ma'am?! Oh geez.

"I apologize, I don't know what to call you."

"Anala."

Her eyes widen as she looks from me to the Priestess and back to me again. "That is really your name? But..."

"Yes, I know, it's all very confusing. All you need to know is I am the true Anala."

Abby's mouth snaps shut before she bows slightly in acknowledgment. "I would like to apologize for Tania. This is not how I would rule this Society, and I see it's not how you would either." Tania begins to argue, and Abby shushes her angrily. "We do not require payment for information. For Tania to request someone who is obviously important to you is beyond reprehensible."

I stare at Abby, trying to gauge her sincerity, and there is nothing but honesty in her eyes. She is either a *really* good liar or she means every word she says. Tania, on the other hand, is behaving like a child having a temper tantrum. Her face is flushed with anger and embarrassment, and I feel my face crack a smile. Okay, so I'm being a little childish myself, but whatever. I almost died, I'm allowed some imprudence, I think.

"Fine. Once Tania stops having her fit, I would like her to discuss Malcolm's plans. I think that it would benefit us all."

"I agree, but she doesn't remember anything."

"I believe my compulsion messed with her memory. She had been drugged by Malcolm, and I think that allowed my coercion to go further than I instructed her."

"May I ask what you compelled her to do?" From the look Abby gives me, it's pure curiosity that makes her ask me the question.

"To forget me and my Hunters."

For the first time, Abby lets her gaze travel over my group. She lingers for a bit on Eric, then comes back to me.

"They are all Hunters?"

"*We* are, yes. Sam and I just happen to be Cursed as well."

Abby nods. "Tania, you need to tell... Anala what Malcolm's plans are."

"You're not my Ruler!"

Abby spins around and grabs Tania's arm so fast that even I'm surprised by the movement.

"You will watch your tongue with me! You know very well I outrank you! I will not rule as the Priestess did. I will not kill you. But I will not hesitate to extricate you from the Society if you do not help us counter whatever Malcolm is planning."

Impressive. That's the first word that comes to mind when I listen to Abby's little speech. She would make a good leader. Sam squeezes my shoulder silently in agreement. I notice that Monica stays out of it, which to me means she is quietly choosing to give her loyalty to Abby.

There's a silent standoff between Abby and Tania before Tania finally lowers her gaze, effectively surrendering to Abby's authority.

"He has been rallying allies for a while now. Men who oppose the idea of being ruled by women."

"We know this already," I interrupt impatiently. "What we need to know is when he is planning this little revolution and how he has managed to control everyone, including Cursed Ones."

Ooo, if looks could kill, I'd be a speck of dust from one look from Tania. Deep down, I enjoy that I'm getting under her skin.

"Drugs mostly," Tania reveals. "That's how he manipulates the humans. I just never thought he was doing it to me, too. He gets them addicted, then promises them more if they devote themselves to his cause. If they don't get addicted, he uses brute force. Gunner and the others force them into submission with guns and fists. As for the Cursed Ones, he provides them with...meals. That is what he uses most of the true Rulers for. Women are his pawns to control the vampires around us. He doesn't really care about the others or if they get to rule their territories. The only thing he cares about is being like the Priestess."

I glance at the deceased 'Priestess.' I doubt he wants to end up like her now. However, if he's not careful, that's exactly where he's headed.

"Alright, we know the who, what, how, and why. Now, tell me when."

"There is or was supposed to be a ceremony of sorts for the Priestess."

"That's right!" Abby interjects. "She was to choose her mate who would, well, hopefully, impregnate her with a daughter."

"Jesus." I can't believe this stuff was actually happening here. What on earth was Emma thinking, doing this? Maybe I'll get to ask her before I have to kill her.

Jenna practically chokes on her gum. "Eww, that's just wrong."

Abby shrugs. "It was tradition. It seems that tradition has been...terminated."

"When is this 'celebration' supposed to have taken place?"

"On the night of the Blood Moon."

"That's two nights from now."

Abby walks past my watchful Hunters and stops in front of me. "Yes. I would like to help. Whatever you need, my loyalty belongs to you."

"How could you do that, Abby?! It is because of her that our Priestess is dead!"

"It is because of the *true* Anala that *you* are alive, Tania," Abby retorts. "She saved your life, as well as mine and Monica's. She deserves my loyalty far more than the Priestess ever did."

Monica breaks her silence and steps forward. "I agree. My loyalty belongs with the true Anala."

To my surprise, the surviving Hunters and the Cursed Ones who made it through the battle all step forward and declare their allegiance to me. All except Tania.

I raise an eyebrow. "Are you aligning yourself with your brother, Tania?"

She doesn't answer immediately, and I wonder if that's exactly what she will do.

"I stand behind Abby," she finally answers, dismissing me and my authority. Unfortunately, she also allows herself to leer at Sam, who is standing behind me.

"I do not care who you stand behind, Tania, as long as it is on the right side." I ignore Tania for a moment, turning to Abby. "We need to meet somewhere other than here to make plans. Amanda will tell you where to meet. We have to finish things here, and then we will be able to leave as well."

"Do you need help?"

"No. Thank you, but we will take care of this. Emma and I have a history. It is up to me to put it to rest."

"Very well. You heard her," she shouts. "Let's get moving!"

Amanda gives Abby the address where we're staying, and they all start to file out.

"Tania!" My loud voice cuts through the chatter, and she halts in mid-step, turning back to me with a sour look. "One more thing."

Silently, I walk closer to her. She doesn't see it coming. No one else does either, if the collective gasps are an indication when I punch Tania.

"I pulled my punch this time." I kneel beside Tania, who is bleeding profusely from her nose. "But do not be so stupid as to think I'll be as considerate next time. Sam will *never* be yours. For your sake, be careful when you're around us again. Do you understand?"

Tania shrinks back from my menacing stare and nods. She then clambers to her feet and runs away.

CHAPTER TWENTY-ONE

"GOTCHA."

"Are you ready for this, Ana?" Eric and Emily have secured Emma's arms with silver chains. I'm not worried about her overpowering me or my Hunters, but honestly, I'm just not in the mood to fight her. All I want is to be done with all of this.

"Let's get it over with."

"You know, we could just...not take the stake out," Amanda suggests.

"Kill her while she's paralyzed?"

"Ana, we have her secured with silver. I mean, will there be a difference? At least this way you won't have to talk to her. Or hear her say something you may not want to hear."

I'm weary enough to consider Amanda's suggestion. What more could I really get from Emma? And if there is more, do I want to know? How blissful was my ignorance before Bernard returned to my life? Of course, I wouldn't trade my time with Sam for anything, but that doesn't mean I have to expose myself to more. Do I owe Emma anything? No. I don't owe her anything. I barely knew the girl. Her parents thought they could own me, Thomas became someone I hated, and Emma herself used her reputation to spread fear among the Society. She killed innocents, maybe even her own children.

"You're right. She has nothing to say that I want to hear. Remove the chains," I instruct Eric. "Then step out, and I will finish this."

"Ana, no." Jenna confidently approaches me, and I see nothing but compassion in her eyes. "You made us turn around for Zac, and you were too distraught over Sam when you killed Thomas to let us in. You can't keep shutting us out of the things that hurt you the most."

"Jenna is right, Ana. We know you're our leader, but I think of us more like a family." Emily steps next to Jenna. "I lost it when Zac...but you let me rave. You let me come after you. You let me stab you, even though I knew you only did what you had to do. You were there for me. For us. It's our turn to be here for you."

"Why don't you just let me do it, A? She's Cursed. It's what I'm trained for," Jeremy offers.

Let him, baby.

I glance at Sam, seeing the drawn look on his face. Sigh.

"Get it done, and let's get out of here."

"Oh my God, I need a dang shower!" Amanda drops her weapons on the floor inside the door as if she were kicking off her shoes.

We opted to come back to the house we've been renting while here. I felt it would be better for my Hunters to be as comfortable as possible before facing Malcolm.

"I think we could all use a shower," I quip, looking down at my bloody self.

"I need food." Jenna stops dropping weapons all around her when I'm sure she feels all of our eyes on her. "What?"

"How do you eat so damn much?"

"Oh, come on! We haven't eaten since this morning, Ana! I'm starving!"

"But you had like ten pancakes this morning. Plus eggs, bacon, ham..."

"Yeah, yeah. And then I used a lot of energy trying to keep my ass alive. I worked all that food off. I need more."

I can't help but chuckle at her. She's right. We all expelled a lot of energy trying to stay alive. "Fine. Order whatever you want, then go take a shower. Deliveries never make it here under thirty minutes, so you'll have time." I give her a mischievous look. "Believe me, you need it. You wouldn't want to offend the delivery guy, would you?"

Jenna laughs. "Bitch."

Smiling, I choose to ignore her pet name for me. "We can talk about what happened tonight if you guys want. If not, we can wait. It's up to you." I intertwine my fingers with Sam's. "Get cleaned up. We'll all feel much better after that."

It doesn't go unnoticed by me that Sam has been extremely quiet during the ride back to the house, and even while we walk to our bedroom. Not even his thoughts are coming through to me. I decide to wait until we're alone before confronting him, and as soon as the door is closed, I turn to him.

"Talk to me, baby. You're shutting me out again."

Sam rests his hands on my hips, leaning close until his forehead touches mine. "I don't mean to shut you out, sweetheart. Perhaps fear is what keeps my mind closed to you."

I pause to enjoy the endearment. It's one he hasn't used before, and it sounds nice coming from his lips. Then I think about the other thing he said. Fear. Could that really be what keeps his mind closed off to mine? It'll be something to explore at some point.

"What are you afraid of?"

"Look at you, Anala. You're covered in blood. *Your* blood. I held you in my arms as it poured from your neck. *You weren't healing.*" The last part was said as barely a whisper.

"Baby, I'm here. I'm right here."

"I saw that blade coming at you, and there was nothing I could do."

"You warned me, and I was able to move in time to avoid permanent damage." I try to downplay it as much as I can for Sam's sake, but I don't think it's working very well.

"I don't know what I would have done if..."

"Sam, don't think about that," I softly interrupt. "If you dwell on what might have been, you'll get distracted if we face another battle. That could be deadly for both of us, baby. You need to let what happened tonight go."

"I don't know if I can do that."

I grab Sam's hand and lead him to the bed, nudging him until he is seated. Without hesitation, I sit astride his lap and take his face in my hands.

"When you were hurt by Thomas, lying there in the hospital dying, I wanted to die with you. I wasn't there to help you, to warn you, to protect you. The guilt of that weighed heavily on me. When I initially turned Amanda down after she asked me to change you, I think I went a little crazy." I kiss him softly before continuing. "I'm realizing that if we're going to do this, we need to trust each other enough to take care of ourselves. Otherwise, we're both in serious trouble."

"Intellectually, I know you're right. Emotionally, it's a little more difficult to get used to."

"For me, too," I confess. "But we'll give it our best shot, right?"

Sam chuckles. "Right. First thing on the agenda, a shower." He stands, and my legs instinctively wrap around his waist, while my arms go around his neck. "I don't like seeing all of this blood on you. And, we have some unfinished business to take care of," he says, wiggling his eyebrows seductively.

A wide grin spreads across my face. "Yippie!"

"Jenna, when I said to order whatever you want, I didn't mean order all of the food in England."

"I couldn't figure out what I wanted, so I got a little bit of everything." She shrugs and stuffs half an egg roll in her mouth.

A 'little bit of everything' includes Chinese take-out, pizza, sushi, Thai, and even some kind of fried chicken. Amazingly enough, I have no doubts that my small group of six Hunters (excluding the two vampires, since Sam and I don't need the food) can polish off every last bit of this food.

"How are you feeling?" Amanda shoots a glance at me, then Sam. Whatever she sees prompts a sly smile. "Pretty good, I guess."

"I'm good," I grin, then turn serious. "How about all of you? Anything you want to talk about?"

"I'm assuming you want to know if we had to kill any innocents. Correct?"

"Yes, Eric." I need to know. I don't want to know, but I need to.

"I didn't," Eric answers immediately, and looks to Jeremy.

"Nope. Jenna?"

"Not me. Emily?"

"No. Sara?"

"No, I didn't. Amanda?"

I'm finding this 'around the table' confession quite entertaining until Amanda remains quiet.

"Amanda?" The concern in Sam's voice makes me as nervous as Amanda's silence.

"I-I don't know. Everything happened so fast."

I place my hand over hers. "What happened?"

I was fighting with a Cursed One, and suddenly, this girl appears out of nowhere. Ana, she couldn't have been more than fifteen. I tried my best to fend her off without hurting her, but the Cursed One kept coming after me. I just needed her to leave me alone so I could handle the vamp for her sake as well as mine. I hurt her. I don't know how badly, but I did. She pauses to take a deep breath. "I never went back to find out what happened to her. By that time, you had been hurt, and my attention was on you."

Standing, I pull Amanda up with me and hug her. "You did what you had to do, Mandy Bear," I murmur, using Sam's nickname for her. "I'm sure she's fine, but if not, you did what you were trained to do. You said the same thing to me when defending Liam, remember? We can't save everyone. You protected yourself."

She nods, and I hear her sniffle softly. I lift my eyes to Sam. He immediately stands up and wraps Amanda in his arms.

"She's right, Mandy Bear. Someone very smart told me that we need to take everything from tonight and let it go. Otherwise, we'll be distracted the next time this happens."

Amanda sighs. "Let me guess. Ana told you that because you're having a hard time seeing her like she was tonight?"

"Yes."

"I think we all did," Amanda admits, turning her head to look at me. "You're our formidable leader. Seeing you go down like that was a real eye-opener. One I'd rather forget."

"So forget it," I tell all of them. "Easier said than done, I know, but it's necessary. I'm sorry it happened, believe me, but it did. I'm fine, and now it's time to move on and prepare for the next battle. Honestly, I hope this is the last one for a *long* time, if not forever. I'm ready for retirement."

You're definitely old enough," Jenna teases. I take it as it is—a way to lighten the mood that had become way too gloomy. So, instead of smacking Jenna for her dig about my age, I steal her piece of pizza and stick my tongue out at her.

After spending the rest of the night reassuring Sam that I am okay, I wake up feeling remarkably refreshed when morning breaks through. The weather is a bit more like typical England today—overcast with sporadic showers. It doesn't matter, though, since we'll be spending the day indoors training.

Sam and I walk into the gym together, noticing everyone is already there. I stop for a moment to watch them spar with each other. Respect grows inside me as I see how well they work together and how much they've improved in such a short time. There are other feelings there too—love and a sense of belonging. God, it's been so long since I've had family that I'd forgotten what that felt like.

"We *are* your family, baby."

Sam's breath tickles my ear and makes me shiver, as does the finger he trails lightly down my sports bra-clad back. Clearing my throat, I grab his hand and drag him to the center of the room.

"Let's go, hotshot." I raise my hands, palms up, and beckon him to come at me. It's either spar with him or drag him back to our bedroom. The sensible part of me has won over, and he's going to have to deal with the consequences of stirring up my need for him.

"Something wrong, sweetheart?" he smirks.

"Not at all, *darling*."

"You sure?"

"You stalling?"

He laughs. "Let's do this."

By this time, my Hunters have stopped sparring and are now watching us with amusement. Sam circles me for a step or two, then strikes out at me. He knows I'll be ready for it, so he tries countering with a sweep of my legs. I'll admit, he almost had me.

"Not bad." I grin. This is beginning to remind me of one of the first times we sparred after becoming lovers. He tried knocking me off balance by saying something seductive. Unfortunately for me, it had worked. My grin spreads wider.

I want to make love to you again.

Sam's eyes widen, and he falters ever so slightly. As he did with me at that time, I use it against him, grabbing him and spinning him around until my breasts are pressed against his back.

"Gotcha."

"Dirty move," he murmurs huskily with laughter. Seems he remembers that moment just as clearly as I do.

"Doesn't make it untrue," I say, repeating his past words to me.

"You guys aren't going to suck face, are you?"

I give her a mock glare. "Jenna, you really know how to ruin a moment."

"Get over it. It's not like you two don't have forever to get it on." *Pop.*

I fantasize about taking her gum and wrapping it through the strands of her braid. She'd have to shave her head by the time I was done. Sam laughs out, then laughs even harder when Jenna looks at him in confusion.

Hey, at least it's getting their minds off of more morbid thoughts. I'll take it.

CHAPTER TWENTY-TWO
"I BELIEVE IN YOU."

"I appreciate you coming out here to meet with us, Abby." I also appreciate the fact that she didn't bring Tania along, but I'll keep that to myself.

"Of course, Anala. It's an honor..."

"Please don't do that. I'm nothing like your Priestess, or Emma. I don't want or need your adulation. Once I'm finished here, that's it."

"You're not staying to rule over us?"

"No. I'm not your Ruler. England already has a queen, and you certainly don't need another Priestess. I am a Leader of my own chapter of the Society. That's where I belong."

"But you could come back here," Abby starts.

"I don't *want* to come back," I interrupt. "I don't want this life anymore. Look, I have no idea what is going to happen with Malcolm tomorrow. In fact, I'm afraid it's going to be our toughest battle yet because of the innocents that will be involved. But no matter the outcome, this is it for me, Abby."

"You were born a Hunter. How could you leave this life behind?"

"Honestly, I did very well for many centuries. Blissfully unaware of the things that were happening here in my home country. Now, all I really want is to spend the rest of eternity with Sam. Preferably on a beach somewhere, sipping margaritas and being happy."

Sam places his hand on the small of my back, rubbing it gently. I don't know if he wants what I want or if he'd get bored with that life. Maybe he wants to be a cop again. It's not impossible, just a bit doubtful that a life as a cop would work for long periods. He would have to keep starting over in different parts of the world because of not aging. I should have probably talked this over with him.

Hell, I probably should have talked this over with my Hunters before mentioning it to Abby. Surely they want more out of life than just killing Cursed Ones. They had dreams before I arrived. It's time they started living for themselves, not for me or the Society.

"Very well. I respect your decision, actually. Had I thought I had any other choice, I wouldn't have chosen this life either."

"You were forced into it?"

"Anala, I don't know where you came from or what happened before you got here. The fact that you didn't know this was happening seems strange to me. But around here, we're still born to be Hunters. Our families still practiced, trained, and protected. It's not that I was forced — it's simply what I was born into. What is expected of me. I'm sure you, of all people, understand that."

I nod, knowing exactly what she was talking about. My Hunters, although technically born Hunters, had no knowledge of this life before me. They didn't have to make the sacrifices or spend their youth training to become killers. The truth is, they've only scratched the surface of what someone like Abby or myself has had to go through. Of course, I never complained when I was younger. It was something sacred to me. Then again, I grew up with mum and papa, two truly remarkable, generous, and understanding Leaders. Growing up with someone like the Priestess is clearly enough to take the fun out of anything.

We've ordered food again because, honestly, who in this group is going to cook? I can cook, mind you, but have you seen the way Jenna eats? So, we're now on a first-name basis with the delivery people around here, and we've been here less than a week. Damn. Has it really been less than a week? It feels like we've been here or been fighting for ages. I'm so tired of it. Clearly, this isn't the life for me anymore. I've come to realize there are more important things out there. Love is something my parents and I never really discussed. Of course, they loved me, and I loved them, but I'm talking about being in love. Maybe I wasn't ready for how being in love with Sam would make me feel about my life, or how it has been. But ready or not, it's here to stay, and I want to make the most of this love.

I shake my head mentally, trying to focus on the task at hand. I've never been prone to getting lost in deep thoughts. Then again, I've never almost had my head chopped off while the love of my life watched. It tends to change your outlook on life. Sigh.

"Did the Priestess know anything about Malcolm's plan to overthrow her?" I take a sip from my bottle of blood, silently thanking Amanda for making sure to use an opaque bottle. I'm sure Abby suspects what's in the bottle, but that doesn't mean I have to advertise it.

"She knew of the rumors, but no specific plans. She usually brushed them off, too vain to believe anyone could take her command away from her."

I hand the shrimp with lobster sauce to Abby since she's been eyeing it for a while now.

"I take it she didn't have any plans to circumvent Malcolm's advance?"

Abby shakes her head, covering her mouth with her hand as she chews. If I had asked Jenna a question after she had taken a bite, I would have seen everything she had crammed into her mouth. Sam snickers softly, and I bump his shoulder. I wonder if he's been listening to all my inner ramblings.

Yes. We will talk about things later.

Sounds ominous. He just smiles at me, winking a sexy little wink. Damn him. Now I want to...

"No," Abby finally answers after swallowing her food, effectively bringing me out of my wayward thoughts. "She believed she had enough protection from her subordinates, including Cursed Ones. She wasn't worried."

"And what do you think?"

My Hunters have been unusually quiet since Abby arrived, so I'm caught off guard when Amanda asks the question. It must have been the same for Abby, as she hesitates with a glance at me before answering.

"I think we have a reason to be worried. It's Amanda, right?"

"Yes."

"I apologize. We're here eating together, and I haven't made an effort to speak with all of you."

See? I *told* you my mind was occupied elsewhere! I should have made introductions the moment Abby stepped in the door.

"My apologies for my bad manners," I say sheepishly. "Abby, these are my Hunters, my friends, my family; Amanda, Jenna, Emily, Sara, Jeremy, and Eric. And, of course, Sam."

"Eric, are you and Emily related?"

Interesting that she singles out Eric. I remember her gaze also lingering on him at the Priestess's hideout. Hmm.

"Yes. We're twins," Eric responds, a slight blush forming on his cheeks. I don't think I've ever seen Eric flustered before. Hmm, again.

"Wow. And what is your strength?"

It is true that each Hunter is born with qualities, or strengths, that make them powerful Hunters. When I first recruited my group, I made it a point to let each of them know what theirs was. Eric's and Emily's were quite obvious to me.

"Swordsmanship. Emily and I are master fencers."

"That's wonderful." Abby hesitates again, her eyes lingering on Eric a bit longer than polite, then she smiles at Emily before turning to Jeremy. Her hesitation makes me wonder if she had intended to ask any of the others.

"And yours?"

Jeremy clears his throat, clearly not expecting to be part of this conversation. "Um, brute strength and ability to think under pressure," he answers, almost verbatim repeating what I told him. At least I know he was listening.

"Fantastic qualities. And Jenna?"

Jenna's fork stops in mid-air, and she looks annoyed with the interruption. Okay, yes, Jenna *always* looks annoyed.

"Maneuverability," she answers dryly. "And bitchiness."

I laugh, just like the rest of my group. Abby doesn't seem as entertained by the answer as the others do. Oh well, she'll either get used to Jenna or not. She is an acquired taste, after all.

"Hmm. Sara?"

Sara looks at her with confusion on her face. Oops. Since Sara was a latecomer, I never got the chance to meet her or tell her what her qualities are. However, if I had to guess...

"Sara's quality is compassion," I reply. "She came to us late in the game, so I never had the chance to discuss this with her." Turning to face Sara, I say, "Each Hunter has a trait that makes them excel at what they do. We're still getting to know each other, but I can see your strength is compassion. You also have a strong sense of right and wrong, and duty. Your compassion keeps you grounded, but your sense of duty keeps you alive. It's a very powerful combination."

Sara blushes at my words, and I hope that's a good thing because I definitely meant it as a compliment.

"Gracias."

"Those are brilliant qualities," Abby agrees. "You don't see much of that around here anymore. Under the Priestess, most Hunters have lost their compassion. What about you, Amanda?"

"I have, um, uh..." Amanda looks at me. It's almost as if she still doesn't believe what I told her about her qualities. I give her a brief nod, and she swallows nervously. "The ability to retain all of these abilities," she mechanically recites word-for-word what I said to her that night.

"Truly?" Abby's eyes widen, and she looks to me for confirmation.

"Yes," I nod. "Both she and Sam possess the power to retain all abilities. Including being able to sense Cursed Ones."

"That's almost unheard of in these areas. In fact, I've never met a Hunter who could sense." Abby shakes her head, apparently in amazement. "Wait. How do all of you know each other if Hunters were not typical in your area, and how did you survive them, Anala?"

"They met in high school," Sam replies, gesturing toward the others. "As for Anala, even if we had known what Cursed Ones were before she told us, we can't sense her."

"You can't... but she is Cursed."

"Anala is, by her own account, an anomaly. She never went through what other Cursed Ones experienced when they were turned."

"Neither have you, Sam," Amanda reminds him.

"It is quite remarkable how... civilized you both are," Abby states. "Your voices are absolutely clear. If it weren't for your eyes, I would never have imagined you were Cursed. I've never seen that before."

I shrug. Hell, I can't explain it now any more than I could centuries ago. I don't know why the evil didn't consume me. I'm just glad it didn't, even more so with Sam.

"This is all so fascinating. My parents would have never believed this."

"Are they still here?"

Abby frowns and then looks at me with sad eyes. "No. They did not conform to the rules of the Priestess, wanting instead to follow the guidelines of your parents. They were sentenced to death for treason. I wish I could have killed the Priestess myself, but I couldn't."

Intuitively, I understand she couldn't because it went against her nature as a Hunter. That is a sign of a true Hunter. Even after her parents' death, she wouldn't harm the Priestess because she was human. Knowing what happened to Abby's parents, and why, makes me less sad that Liam killed the Priestess now.

"I'm sorry for your loss, Abby," I say sincerely. "I know nothing will make it better, but at least now you know you don't have to live under the Priestess's rules any longer."

"Yes. That actually makes it a bit better, though it's still scary. We're so used to being under someone's rule, I'm not sure what the Hunters will do now."

"*You* become their Leader."

She drops her fork and sits back in her chair, eyes wide with disbelief. "Me!? I'm not a Leader!"

"Of course you are. You do realize that those who left with you today are loyal to you. They will follow your lead. Be good to them. Show them how a true leader should be. Faith in the Society will be restored, and with a few tweaks to the rules, this land could live in harmony."

"You really think I could lead as your parents did? They are still legendary here, you know. The Priestess tried to quell the stories about them, but they never stopped. That leadership is what Hunters wanted again."

"So give it to them. I believe in you."

"It's rightfully yours, Anala. You are their daughter."

"I told you, Abby, I don't want it. Do any of you?" I ask my Hunters. Heads are vehemently shaking with emphatic "nos". "There you have it. You know this land and these people. They know and trust you, it seems. Lead them. Fix this mess, Abby."

"That's not a daunting request at all," she sighs.

Laughing, I place my hand on her shoulder. "It *is* daunting, but we're here to help you get started. First, we need to develop a plan for Malcolm that will result in as few casualties as possible. Now *that's* troublesome. Are you all ready?"

The room fills with unenthusiastic "yesses." I understand the feeling. I just hope this isn't an impossible task.

CHAPTER TWENTY-THREE
"CUT OFF THE HEAD."

"I don't suppose Malcolm would be open to talking out our problems?"

Ah, Eric. Ever the diplomat. "Since Abby is taking over, he's not going to be any happier than he was with the Priestess," I answer with a smile. "His ego far exceeds his intellect."

"I agree," Abby also sends Eric a smile that makes him blush. "I have tried talking to him on behalf of the Priestess. God, I hate calling her that. I've always thought it was an obnoxious title, but it doesn't seem right to call her Anala."

I shudder. "It's way too weird for me having another Anala out there."

"Not anymore," Jenna points out. "You're the only one again, Ana. I don't think you have to worry about it anymore."

"Right. Okay, let's figure this Malcolm thing out. Abby, you said that you tried talking to him. What did you say?"

"It was more of a threat," Abby sighs. "That's what I was told to do. I tried telling him that he could continue to rule his territory *if* he followed the Priestess. If he chose to continue with this revolution, we would have no choice but to *rid* ourselves of our problem. But he refused. He wanted more. He wanted what the Priestess had."

"He should be careful what he wishes for," Emily said softly.

She's right, of course. If he decides to continue with this fight, he'll lose just like my namesake did. Not only is that bad for him, but it's also bad for my Hunters. Amanda was clearly upset at the thought of hurting an innocent. If she kills someone without a doubt, I'm not sure how that will affect her. Or any of them. Unless I can persuade Malcolm to change his mind, there's nothing I can do to protect my friends. They will never let me go through with this without their support.

"Tania said that Malcolm deals with drugs. Is that his main business?"

"Yes. I think Tania was right about that being how he controls his Enforcers. They're not even Hunters. At least not all of them. A fight with them would be highly uneven and dangerous for us all."

"Because of the guns?" Amanda glances at me, and I see her glare of defiance. Like she's daring me to tell them they can't be part of this fight. Oh, how I want to do just that.

"Yes. They don't play fair," Abby answers. "Meaning, they're not above placing gunmen strategically where none of us will see them."

"Like snipers?" Sam sits up straighter, suddenly more interested in the conversation. He had been quiet until now, just taking everything in. I can feel the fear and apprehension flowing through him at the mention of hidden gunmen.

"Yes. They're not exactly skilled because he doesn't use the Hunters as snipers."

That could be even more dangerous," Sam says as he stands and begins his trademark Logan pacing. This doesn't bode well for Amanda and the others.

"What if we try to work out a deal with him concerning the drugs?" Abby suggests. "We promise to provide for him, if he promises to..." Sam's low growl cuts her off.

Sam was a cop," I say, watching him intently. My eyes flick back and forth. Back and forth. "And, even if he wasn't, I don't like the idea of using drugs. In fact, I want that stopped. You should too, since you'll be leading the Hunters in this area. Drugged-up Hunters aren't exactly reliable.

Abby sighs. "I know. I just don't know what else to do that will cause the least amount of bloodshed."

"We have," I glance at the clock above the fireplace, "less than twenty hours to come up with something."

"Could you compel Malcolm to order the others to stand down?" Sara asks.

I consider the possibilities for a moment, then shake my head. "I'm afraid I would have to compel all of the 'rulers' of the Enforcers. Malcolm may have arranged this plan, but I don't believe he has full control. Do you?" I ask Abby.

She shakes her head. "There's a group, according to Tania. They have meetings to discuss their plan of action."

"Did Tania hear any of those actual plans?"

Abby looks at me apologetically. "Tania isn't exactly the best source of information. She tends to overdramatize things to the point where I'm unsure what's real and what's her imagination. Though now that I know she was being drugged by Malcolm, I guess I can understand that."

"Great," I mutter. "So, we have a power-hungry group, drugged-up Hunters and innocents, and Cursed Ones that are willing to follow them because they are promised all the blood they want. Oh yeah, not to mention guns." I stand and start pacing along with Sam.

What are we going to do, Sam? They could get hurt if we go into this fighting.

I know. Sam runs his hand through his hair. *I won't allow Amanda to get hurt. Or any of the others. If I have to tie them down, I will.*

Yeah, that will go over real well.

"It'd be nice if we could just cut off the head of the snake."

I stop in mid-step, causing Sam to run into me. But I move to the side and let him continue while Jenna's nonchalant suggestion sparks something in my mind. Cut off the head. What if we could do just that? It certainly works with Cursed Ones.

I turn to Abby. "How many heads are there?"

Abby pauses for a moment. I imagine she's counting. "There are six from different regions. Ireland, Scotland, Spain, the Netherlands, Northern Ireland, and here."

"Do you know if they're going to meet before they travel to my hometown?"

"I would imagine they're going to in order to go over strategy. What are you thinking?"

"I'm thinking that Jenna had a good idea, as crazy as that sounds."

"Hey! I resemble that remark!" Jenna smirks. "Wait, what was my idea?"

Amanda and the others look at her as if she's a little crazy. I can't help but laugh at her. "Cut the head off the snake, Jenna. The 'Enforcers' and Cursed Ones look to the Head—or in this case, Heads—for guidance. If we take that away from them, or at least lead them to a different head, like Abby, hopefully we can get out of this with the least amount of bloodshed," I finish with Abby's words.

"So, we, what? Kill Malcolm and the other rulers?" Jenna asks seriously.

"I hope it won't come to that, but if it does, you and the others will *not* be involved." I raise my hand as they all begin arguing at once. "Please! These are *armed humans*. Amanda, you are devastated thinking about hurting that innocent, and you don't know what really happened. What will happen if you actually *do* knowingly kill someone?"

Amanda's mouth snaps shut, tears welling in her eyes. Of course, I feel horrible for doing that to her, but if this is the only way for them to understand the consequences of fighting me, it's something I have to do. But, God, it hurts seeing her like this.

I'm sorry, Amanda," I whisper, watching Sam go to her and wrap his arm around her.

She understands you're just trying to keep her safe, baby.

She may understand, but I don't think she will forgive me for throwing it in her face like that. Sigh.

Abby clears her throat lightly. "I can tell you from personal experience that taking the life of an innocent is not something you want to live with," she tells Amanda softly. "Even when it was done *only* because you had no other option besides your own death. Sometimes you wonder, on those darkest days, if you should have chosen your own death instead."

Abby is probably no older than twenty-five if I'm judging right. For someone that young to have endured such a depressing life is unacceptable to me. Emma has done nothing but destroy lives and turn the Society into a joke. It irritates me that my parents' legacy has become this way because of greed and ego. I will put an end to this here.

I place my hand on Abby's forearm as a gesture of support and condolence. Then I let go and take Amanda's hand in mine. "I don't know if I've ever been clear about how much you mean to me. You are like the sister I never had. I felt a connection with you right away, and I never understood why, but I didn't question it. I didn't want this to be your life, Amanda. Believe me, if I could have found another way to do this, I would have. I should have," I correct myself. "I should have dug deeper, looked harder for other Hunters, but I didn't. You're here. All of you are here, your lives in danger because of me. Do you really think I'd be able to live an eternity if something happened to you? Any of you? You all mean a great deal to me. Let me protect you."

I don't think you looked harder because you knew you could only trust us. Your secret couldn't have stayed hidden forever, Ana," Amanda tells me softly. "You must have known that deep down, and trusted us. Even Jenna." Amanda gently bumps Jenna's shoulder when Jenna glares at her.

"Maybe," I smile. "And maybe I need to let you help. In" I hurry and continue when Sam's eyes snap to mine, "a very-far-away-from-the-guns way."

"Meaning?" Sam asks irritably. Man, when he disagrees with me, he certainly isn't shy about letting it show.

"Meaning they can patrol the area in the woods, Sam. We have yet to see innocents out there. Only Cursed Ones."

"This close to a fight, how do you know they won't be out there now making sure none of the Priestess's people are out spying?" he counters.

"You and I will know if innocents are there. If your *theory* is right, then we'll change our plans." I glance at Abby again, trying to quell my annoyance with Sam. This 'tug-of-wits' between us is starting to feel too much like when we first met, and he thought he would control everything. "I'm, of course, assuming that the meeting will take place at Malcolm's?"

"It's the closest place to the Priestess's hideaway, so yes. His innocents don't usually patrol so close to his house. I'm guessing it's because cops have been there a few times for drug-related issues. Cursed Ones can make the cops forget and get a meal out of it. Humans are too flawed, according to Malcolm. He's afraid they will give him up if pressured enough."

I force myself not to give Sam a smug look. But I quickly realize that it doesn't matter if he doesn't see it if he can hear my damn thoughts. Sam storms out of the room angrily with one thought that I don't want to repeat. Shit. We definitely don't have time for us to be fighting each other.

"Okay, the plan for now is that all of you will patrol the woods. That includes you, Abby. If you feel you need more manpower, bring only those you trust. Leave Tania at home, please. I don't need that distraction." Abby nods, and I continue. "If Malcolm's Cursed Ones are out there, don't hesitate to take them out. They use humans for food, and I'm pretty sure they don't care if they die or not. They will not be considered for reprieve like Liam and his group. Sam and I—if he's speaking to me—will have a chat with Malcolm and the others and make sure they see our way of things."

"And, if they don't?" Jeremy asks.

"They won't have a choice," I reply firmly. "This war is pointless. Innocents are getting killed, drugged, or used as feeders for Cursed Ones, either without their knowledge or out of fear for their lives. If the greater good means eliminating a few bad people, I will do what is necessary."

I don't look any of my Hunters in the eye as I say that. It shames me to think that I would consider murdering an innocent. I hope to come up with an alternative method with Sam later.

"For now, you all need to rest. Please, get some sleep. I need you all to be extremely alert tomorrow for whatever may happen. If cutting off the head does nothing but grow another head, we're in trouble." I pause to think, already tweaking my plan as thoughts come to me. "Abby, set up people at the hideout. Make sure they're out of sight and make it clear that we will only fight if it is a last resort."

Abby nods, typing something on her phone. "I'm making a list of people to bring with me, and people to send there," she explains when I give her a questioning look. "I assume Liam is trustworthy if you're offering him reprieve?"

"Yes. Make sure your people know they are not to be harmed. Amanda, I need you to make sure Liam knows who's on the good side."

"Got it."

"I want half of you in the woods, and the other half at the hideout. I need people I trust to be able to yell out orders and ensure they're carried out." I'm really just flying by the seat of my pants with the plans right now. It's all I can do with such short notice and limited intel. Normally, I would prefer to recon the situation for at least a week before diving into something like this. But we do what we have to do as leaders, and we hope to all that is good in the world that what you're doing is what's best and will keep everyone alive. "I'm going to go talk to Sam. We'll review and refine the plan further tomorrow. For now, go rest. Abby, you're more than welcome to stay here. Sara can show you the spare bedroom if you'd like. Let's meet in the dining room at eight a.m. We'll have breakfast and discuss more."

"Pancakes?" Jenna asks excitedly.

"Sure, sounds good. Make a lot," I smirk and wink at her. She sits there stunned, probably thinking about how she just got roped into making everyone breakfast. It is no doubt a *terrible* idea to have Jenna cook for us on such an important day, so I make a note to call someone in the morning to bring food. I'm sure if I pay enough, someone will be willing to deliver breakfast food. "Goodnight, everyone. Get some much-needed sleep. Tomorrow is going to be...interesting to say the least."

"Good luck," Amanda calls out as I head toward a not-happy Sam. I'm going to need it.

CHAPTER TWENTY-FOUR
"GOOD PLAN."

I stop at the door of my and Sam's room and take a deep breath. I haven't felt this much trepidation about seeing Sam since the day he found out what I was and staked me.

Will you ever forgive me for that?

Oh, so you're forcing me out of your head, but still listening in on mine?

He opens the door and stares at me. "I'm not forcing you out, Anala."

Hmm." I push past him, still furious that he left me in the middle of our meeting. I should really calm down before saying anything, but my brain isn't catching on, and before I realize what's happening, I spin around to glare at him. "You do not leave during a meeting as important as this, Sam!"

"The way I was feeling, I needed to get out of there."

"I do not care if your head is about to explode with anger! You suck it up and stay there until I dismiss you!"

"Dismiss me?" he snarls.

"Yes, dismiss! Did you forget I am your Leader? Not only that, I am your Maker! You blatantly disrespected me in there!"

"No, Anala, I didn't forget. But perhaps you forgot I'm also your lover. I thought it was best to leave before I said or did something I would regret." Sam's voice is laced with a venom I've never heard from him before. It creates an acute pain in my chest to hear, and it scares me. Not because I'm afraid of *him*, but afraid of losing him in more ways than one. It really is too bad I'm too angry to reason with myself.

"Being my *lover* does *not* give you permission to disrespect me, Sam."

"And it doesn't give *you* the right to send *my* sister into a situation that could kill her!"

"She's a goddamn Hunter, Sam!" I explode, flinging my arms out in frustration. "*Every* situation could kill her! You don't think that hangs over my head every damn day?! You don't think it hurts my heart that she and the others have had to do things no normal teenager should have to do?! I *trained* them to be assassins, for chrissake! Do you not think I hate myself every damn day for that and for what it has done to them? To *you*?" I swipe angrily at the tear that escapes down my cheek.

Sam's eyes soften, and I want to fight him when he steps closer and wraps his arms around me, but I honestly can't. As weak as you may think it makes me, I allow myself to be held and comforted. It's much better than the alternative, which is losing Sam, risking his humanity, risking our love. We have enough enemies. We shouldn't be that way to each other when we're the only ones who can offer this comfort to the other.

"You gave all of us a choice, Anala. You didn't force us to do this," he murmurs softly.

"That doesn't make it better for me, Sam. It just means you've all trusted me with your lives willingly, and I could make a huge mistake at any given moment to fatally break that trust."

"We knew the risks. And, yes, I realize how hypocritical I'm being right now," Sam sighs, gently blowing his warm breath over the top of my head where his stubbled chin is resting. "Losing Amanda is one of my greatest fears."

"Mine, too," I confess, my voice muffled from my face being buried in his chest. "Not just because I'm her Leader. Sam, she is my family, too. You all are. I lost my parents and have spent centuries alone. You can't seriously think I want to go through that again."

He lifts my chin until I'm looking him in the eye. "I'm sorry. You're right, I shouldn't have disrespected you. Especially in front of everyone. It belittles your authority and demeans our relationship. Forgive me?"

I reach up and brush my lips lightly over his. "If you forgive me for the things I said."

"You said only the truth."

"Sam, I said I didn't care. I *do*. I realize that we can't always say what we're thinking in front of others, but for you to walk away causes more damage than if you stayed and laid it out for me."

"I know. One thing I have noticed that is different about being Cursed; my emotions are way more intense. Unfortunately, that includes my short temper."

"Yes, but it includes other emotions, as well, so I'm not going to complain," I grin.

Sam laughs softly, then turns serious again. "I don't like fighting with you. It literally hurts."

"You felt that, too?"

He takes my hand and lays it over his heart. A steady, strong beat welcomes me, and speeds up a little at my touch.

"It was excruciating. I wonder if that's what it feels like to be staked," he says innocently. It takes me a moment to figure out that he really doesn't grasp what he just said.

"It's close," I deadpan.

He snaps his eyes shut, cursing under his breath. "Baby, I'm . . . "

I quickly silence any apologies by covering his mouth with mine. Enough talking for now. It's time to make up, and then we can talk again.

Good plan.

Here's another. Drink from me.

Sam groans before letting himself make the change and sinking his teeth into my neck.

After making up - and then making up again - Sam and I finally discussed plans for the next day. Turns out, even though Sam was angry, he 'listened' in, so he was much more aware than I expected. He agrees with my tentative plan, which we're about to review with the gang again. The disagreement between us is whether he stays with me or goes to the hideout with the other half of our group. Even though I want nothing more than for him to stay with me, my 'grown-up, responsible' self thinks he should be with the others.

"I'm not going to let you go into that house alone, Anala." Sam is pacing. Again. At least he's not leaving. He shoots me an annoyed glance at that thought.

Sorry. I know we worked that out last night. That was really petty. I silently apologize, sighing in relief when he nods his forgiveness.

"Give me an acceptable alternative, Sam," I say aloud.

"Liam," he answers simply. Which surprises me, actually. I wouldn't have guessed he would trust Liam enough to protect any of our group, especially his sister. "He can be with the group at the hideaway, along with a few of his own. The others can stay back here."

"Okay." It's my turn to surprise Sam by not arguing anymore. I can't. It really is a good plan, and if I'm giving him a chance at staying alive for his loyalty, I might as well let him prove that loyalty once more.

"Okay? Just like that?" Sam asks suspiciously.

"Do you want me to argue more?"

"Can we make up again if you do?" he smirks sexily.

"Ha, ha. And, we can do that without having to fight first," I smile. "Seriously, Liam is a good alternative. The guns won't affect him or anyone in his group, so he'll be able to keep the others safe."

Sam runs his fingertips along my cheek before lifting my chin to kiss me.

"Do you two ever stop?" Jenna bursts into the room with a sandwich and soda.

"Do you?" I ask, looking pointedly at the food.

"Hey, I need food to stay alive, what's your excuse?" She looks at me, then at Sam and back at me. "Never mind." She shakes her head, sits down, and starts eating.

"So, where are we?" Amanda asks, walking in with the others in tow and plopping down in a chair next to Jenna. "Geez, Jenna, didn't you just eat like twenty minutes ago?"

"No, that wa ju a nack," Jenna mumbles around a mouthful. "Need full today."

"Say what?"

She says what she ate earlier was just a snack, and she needs fuel for later today," Jeremy answers lightly.

"Well, what do you know?" I grin. "Jeremy speaks fluent Jenna."

Jeremy blushes furiously, as does Jenna, who decides to stuff more food in her mouth.

Sam clears his throat, and though I don't see a smile on his face, I know he's finding this little episode quite amusing. "Would you all like to go over the plan, or should we keep talking about Jenna's eating habits and Jeremy's uncanny ability to know all things Jenna?"

Okay, I can't help but laugh. Sam is usually a straight-laced guy. When we're alone, he's more relaxed, but around others, he feels he has to be serious. He's the 'adult' of the group, so he thinks it's his responsibility to act that way. So, when he said what he did, with a straight face, it was incredibly funny.

"Plan," Jenna mumbles grumpily.

"Abby, have you learned anything new?" I stifle my laugh and turn to Abby, who has been sitting there taking all of this camaraderie in with a smile. This is how my parents led the Society: with laughter, friendship, and trust. I wonder if that's what Abby is thinking about when she sees us.

"According to my sources, nobody will go to the hideout until the Rulers have had their meeting."

"How reliable are your sources?" Sam asks.

"Reliable enough to want to still have some of our people go to the hideout."

"Hmm. So, Tania?" Yes, I have a mean streak. You would too if some tramp wanted your boyfriend.

"Pretty much. But she doesn't know for sure, which is why I would stick to your original plan. Still, I don't like that we'll be facing guns no matter where we are."

"I don't either," I acknowledge. "That's why we're sending Liam and a few others with the group to the hideout. The rest will stay here. They will be instructed to protect the humans at all costs."

"So, who's going where?" Amanda asks.

"Would you like to decide that on your own, or would you like me to decide?" I ask Amanda sincerely. I could make the decision for them, but I want them to rely on each other. They've done this before, but this could potentially be a much more dangerous situation. I really want to know who they choose to pair together.

"I don't know if we'll be able to decide," Amanda turns to the others. "What do you guys think? I mean, each site could be a possible death trap. How do we choose who goes where?"

"Amanda."

"It's true, Sam. You even got pissed at Ana for suggesting we get involved in this at all." Amanda glares at Sam, making it clear she's unhappy with his behavior last night.

"We worked that all out, Amanda." I glance at Sam apologetically. "And you're right. There are no guarantees that either place will be safe at all. If you choose to stay behind, I won't hold that against you."

"We want to help," Sara assures me. "The guns scare us, but I think that will make us more, um, *cauteloso*?"

"Cautious," I interpret.

"*Sí*. Cautious. There will be Cursed Ones on our side, no?"

"Yes, Liam and his group will help out. I haven't asked Liam yet, but I hope he won't have any issues since he wants the same thing we do: peace in the land.

We will send Liam and some of his group to the hideout with a team, and the rest will stay here."

"Okay, so choose for us," Jenna suggests. "Who stays here?"

Sigh. Obviously, I want to keep Emily and Eric together. Since I've recently realized that Jeremy knows Jenna very well, I think they'll work well together. Now, what about Sara and Amanda? Will Sam be too distracted with Amanda here or far away from him? I glance over at Sam and see him give me a small shrug.

"We'll decide later. Whatever group we choose for the hideout, you'll take Liam and whoever he wants to bring. The others, obviously, will stay here. Abby, pick Cursed Ones you trust and that I would trust my Hunters with. I'll leave your group decision to you, as long as you trust whomever you bring along."

"Got it. I know Cursed Ones who are sympathetic to our cause, meaning they want no part of what Malcolm aims to bring to this land."

"Good. Go and get that set up. Do we have a time frame for the meeting?"

"They will be meeting in two hours."

"And is *that* from a reliable source?"

Abby chuckles. "Yes, that is actually good information. I've had people watching the Rulers, keeping a 'bionic' ear out, so to speak. They'll be ready to move out within the next hour and a half to get to Malcolm's."

"Good. Based on your understanding of how things work here, if we manage to get Malcolm to back off, do you think his subordinates will follow?"

"Yes. They're really nothing more than puppets. It has to come from Malcolm and the other Heads, though. You'll need to get them to tell everyone that they have changed their minds. Can you do that?"

"Oh, don't worry. We'll convince them of the error of their ways."

CHAPTER TWENTY-FIVE
"NO PRESSURE."

A s confident as I was when telling Abby we'd convince Malcolm, standing in the woods now so close to the house, that confidence fades. What if I can't persuade them? What if I have to force them to stand down?

Then we'll deal with that together. Sam declares silently.

I'm grateful not only for his unwavering support but also because he keeps my fears to himself. There's no need for others to realize that, while I'm confident in *their* plan of action, my own remains entirely unclear.

All right, does everyone have their assignments? I make sure my mic is on so the others heading to the hideout can hear me too. After some serious discussion, including a private chat with Sam, we decided to send Amanda and her team to the hideout. It was probably one of the toughest choices Sam and I have made so far. On one hand, having Amanda stay here meant she was close to us but also near what could possibly be a war zone. On the other hand, sending Amanda to the hideout means she is too far away for me to help if something happens to her. We're really hoping no one actually shows up at the hideaway and that we can stop this war before it even leaves Malcolm's place.

We got it, Selene." Amanda's voice sounds cheerful and upbeat, but I notice the faint fear beneath. Good. As I've always said, fear makes them that much more cautious.

"Liam?"

"Here. I'm sorry, who is Selene?"

Amanda's chuckle comes through my earbud.

"I'll explain later," I hear Amanda tell him.

"We're in the woods now," I tell everyone. "Sam and I will head to the house in a minute. Is everything quiet out there?"

Eric, Emily, and Sara are spread out with other members of Liam's group. They all check in with an all-clear, as do Jenna, Jeremy, and Amanda.

"Nothing going on over here, Ana," Amanda's voice comes through clearly. "A few confused people who didn't know that the Priestess's reign was over, but we're letting Abby's people take care of that."

I frown. "Hunters?"

"A little bit of everything, actually. Hunters, Cursed, innocents. The owners of the small motel we stayed at were out here asking what was happening. It seems your namesake's reach went pretty far."

"And we're sure that they're not Malcolm's people trying to get information?"

"Yeah, I'm pretty sure. We'll keep an eye on them, but most of them were pretty shaken up by everything, wondering who was going to protect them from Malcolm."

"So they understand what's happening?"

"They have an idea, probably planted there by the Priestess. She instilled fear in them, telling them she's the only one they can trust. The only one who can keep them safe."

"Gaining their trust," I mumble to myself.

"That's what we're thinking, too. But, as I said, we're letting Abby's team handle that since they'll be the ones sticking around here."

"Good job. Keep the line open, but don't use it unless it's absolutely necessary. I need to be able to concentrate with Malcolm."

"Got it. Good luck. And, Ana?"

"Yes?"

"Stop this before it starts."

Great. No pressure.

"Compel them if you have to," Amanda continues, oblivious to my inner turmoil. "You've compelled large groups before. If Malcolm is as big an ass as we know he is, it may be your only option. No more killing if that's possible."

Amanda's concern is loud and clear. She's still worried about my human-ity. I understand her anxiety, but I'm in a much better place now than I was then. The man I loved was dying, taking my heart with him. Still, having to kill innocents, no matter how despicable they are, is soul-crushing.

"I'll do what I can."

Once again, I find myself standing at the front door of Malcolm's grotesque house, with its hideously ridiculous lion's head door knocker. Yes, I am going in through the front door. I am essentially coming to Malcolm with a peace treaty. Sam and I thought it would be better received if we asked to come in rather than just barging our way in. So, as I did before, I dutifully take the ring of the door knocker and knock three times. And what do you know? There's my old friend, Meathead, looking a little worse for wear. Both of his eyes are black, and he sports a bandaged, black and blue, slightly crooked nose.

"Bitch!"

He takes an angry step towards me, only to be confronted by Sam.

"I don't think so."

Gunner sneers at Sam, clearly confident he can easily beat him. Little does he know.

"Brought a bodyguard this time, didja? Too bad for you, he won't be able to stop me from doing whatever I want to you." Gunner finishes that sentence with a leer at me. Bad move there, Meathead.

I feel the jealous rage build up in Sam, and if I don't nip this in the bud right now, our peace treaty visit will turn into a 'my boyfriend is about to rip your face off' visit.

Baby. Remember why we're here. He can't do anything to me. He can't hurt me. Just let it go.

Sam growls, and the feral sound has Gunner taking a step back. "We're here to see your keeper."

Gunner scowls at Sam's taunt. "You're not welcome here."

"Perhaps you should let Malcolm know we're here," I suggest. Gunner spares me a quick glance before returning his glare to Sam. Perfect. A testosterone stand-off. I so don't have time for this. "Let Malcolm know we're here. *Now.*"

Gunner's eyes jerk to me, conveying confusion before clouding over. He nods, then motions us to come inside.

As we wait for Gunner to fulfill my request, I hold Sam's hand and give it a gentle squeeze.

Are you okay?

Mmm hmm. I think I just felt what you did with Tania. Damn, baby, that was tough.

I know, my love. Let's just get through this, and then we can get away from all of these...

Weirdos? He supplies when I can't find the right one to describe some of the people we've met over the past few days.

"Well, well. If it isn't Ella."

Speaking of weirdos. Malcolm walks in with all the confidence in the world, a small smirk on his face that isn't very attractive. He's dressed in his usual 'I'm the boss' outfit of black leather, guns strapped to each side. His stringy, dyed black hair is pulled back into a ponytail, and I can't help but find him even less appealing than the first time I met him.

"To what do I owe this," his eyes scan my body, lingering on my cleavage much longer than I'm comfortable with, "pleasure."

I run my hand discreetly across Sam's back, hoping to calm him from the fury building inside him.

"First of all, my name isn't Ella," I step toward him, with Sam right behind me. Gunner also moves closer to his position behind Malcolm. "It's Anala."

"Impossible. There is only one Anala, the Priestess," he chokes out the moniker as though it hurts him to call her that. He casually places his right hand on the butt of his gun. "What are you trying to pull?"

"You're right, there *is* only one Anala. Me. I am Anala Geil, daughter of the Leaders of the Society of Hunters."

"Malcolm?"

A stunned Malcolm doesn't notice the others entering the room. He just keeps staring at me. Meanwhile, I make sure to observe our newcomers.

These must be the other 'Heads.' They're all dressed similarly to Malcolm, as if they're ready for a fight. All young, ordinary men, probably in their mid to late twenties. They would blend into society, with nothing about them standing out, and I wonder if that's why they're doing this. Are they playing a dangerous game because they need to feel important and manly? Whatever their reason, they are completely unaware of the very real threat right in front of them.

"Aren't you going to introduce me to your *friends*, Malcolm?"

"You're lying," Malcolm whispers roughly.

"Look at me, Malcolm. Look me in the eye. Am I lying?"

For the first time since meeting Malcolm, he actually looks at me and not at my body. He sees the Cursed eyes and the truth in my words. He wraps his hand around his gun.

"I wouldn't do that if I were you. You know guns won't affect me. And, if you shoot me, you're only going to piss me off. I *really* don't think any of you want that."

"I can just shoot your boyfriend there," Malcolm threatens.

"You could," I answer civilly. "But then he would just be pissed off as well."

Malcolm takes his eyes off me for a moment to look at Sam. His eyes widen when he sees the truth.

"What do you want?"

"For you to stop what you're doing. The Priestess is dead, and your little revolution is unnecessary."

I see Malcolm begin to smile. Wow. This bloke is most definitely not the sharpest tool in the shed if he's thinking what I think he's thinking.

"I won."

Yep. That's what I thought. Sigh.

"No. *I* won. This is *my* home, Malcolm, *my* Society. I do not like what you have done here. I will not allow you to keep doing this to my people." I realize that as I say the words, I truly believe them. While I don't want to stay here and lead these Hunters, they are part of my family. My parents' legacy. I cannot let Malcolm ruin that.

"You think you have authority here? The Society is dead, *Anala*. This is the land of Enforcers now. If you think we're afraid of you, you're wrong. There are seven of us in this room, and only two of you. You're outnumbered."

"Malcolm, don't do this. I'm offering you a chance to move on with your life peacefully." I feel Sam begin his change as he readies for a fight. I am forestalling my own change in hopes that Malcolm will listen to reason.

"Hear that, guys? She thinks she's in control here." Malcolm laughs evilly. "No *woman* will *ever* be in control of me." The others, however, don't share his false mirth. They're eyeing me and Sam warily.

"Perhaps we should listen to her, Malcolm." Based on his accent, I'm guessing he's the leader from the Netherlands. He looks like a typical Nordic with blond hair and sharp features. Nothing about him really stands out. "The Priestess is gone; there's no threat anymore. If it's true and this is the Anala, maybe things can go back to how they were before. Our ancestors were happy with the Society."

Malcolm's eyes darken with anger. I see the moment he makes his decision. He goes for his gun, spins around, aims, and fires at his Netherlands counterpart. Unfortunately for Malcolm, I'm there to take the bullet before anyone even registers that I moved. The bullet rips through my chest as I push the man out of the way. As much as I hate being shot, this couldn't have gone better for me. Malcolm has effectively alienated his once-supporters by trying to kill them.

CHAPTER TWENTY-SIX
"THE SOCIETY WAY."

"You shot at me?!" Netherlands screams.

It really feels like a scene from a bad B-movie western. Malcolm still has his gun drawn, speechless that the man he tried to kill is still alive. Gunner's gun is now out and pointed at me and the other Heads. Their guns are aimed at Malcolm and Gunner. Sam and I share a look as he moves to my side.

Okay? He asks silently.

Hurts like a bitch, but I'm good.

This is quite the development to our advantage.

So it would seem.

"It looks to me, Malcolm, that it is now *you* who is outnumbered," I taunt, knowing full well it will piss him off even more than he is now.

"What are you fools doing? She's just like her disgusting descendant! She wants to rule us, *control* us! She's a woman! Women should not be in a position of authority!" Malcolm is becoming more and more exasperated with each word.

"How positively old-fashioned of you, Malcolm," I say sardonically. "It should not be about the gender of the leader, but the ability. You are clearly *not* qualified."

Malcolm's hand trembles as he raises his gun again. Confident in Sam, I turn my back on Malcolm to face the others. I know, deep down, what this act of defiance will bring. I could have compelled Malcolm and Gunner, but there's no guarantee it would last. We definitely don't want a repeat of this kind of stance.

168

I feel Sam's fingers brush mine, and I know without a doubt he supports my decision.

"I don't know who you are, but I'm pretty sure you want to live peacefully?"

"Yes," Netherlands answers. "I am Roan. My territory is in the Netherlands. The only reason we," he gestures towards his companions, "agreed to Malcolm's demands is because we did not feel the Priestess was fair. It was never about gender." He stammers his explanation as if he's afraid of offending me if he agrees with Malcolm's outlook.

"Weak! You're all weak! I don't *need* you! The Priestess is dead, I have all the support I need without you!" Malcolm screams.

"You don't have the support of our people any longer, Malcolm." This comes from Spain. "Roan is right, the threat is over." He looks to me. "You are really the true Anala?"

"Yes."

"Then you can restore the Society to the way it was?" Scotland asks.

"I can. And I will." I hear Malcolm yell out in frustration, and then rapid gunfire. I feel the bite of multiple bullets as Malcolm and Gunner empty their clips into me and Sam, who moves to me and wraps his arms around me. It's either that or do exactly what Amanda asked us not to do, which is kill Malcolm ourselves.

We didn't need to do anything. After the smoke clears, Malcolm and Gunner's bodies, riddled with bullet holes, lie there unmoving. This is exactly the outcome I expected when I ignored Malcolm's authority. Fortunately, the other Heads are alive and fairly unscathed, with only a few flesh wounds. Apparently, Sam and I make a great shield.

"Ana! Sam! Talk to me!"

I forgot that the mic was on, and Amanda and the others heard everything, including the gunfire.

"We're fine," Sam answers. "That really *does* hurt like a bitch," he murmurs in my ear.

I lean back and take Sam's face in my trembling hands. A first for me. "Are you really okay, baby?" I start checking him over, noticing that the wounds have already healed.

"I am. I promise." Sam kisses me lightly. "Amanda? Everything okay over there?"

"Yes. Sam, are you sure..."

"I'm sure. Anala and I are fine. The other Heads are wounded but fine. Malcolm and Gunner are...gone."

"Dead?"

"Yes."

"Did you?"

"No. Neither I nor Anala did it. They were shot by the others."

I let Sam continue that conversation while I check on my group. Once I'm sure all my Hunters are safe and aware we're safe, I focus on the Heads.

"Are you all alright?"

"Nothing that can't be fixed," Spain replies, looking at me expectantly.

"I won't do that for you. If you have Cursed Ones you trust enough to heal you, I won't stop you. It just won't be me."

"Understood. I am Miguel. My territory is in Spain." He thrusts his blood-covered hand out, then sheepishly apologizes for the mess. He has dark olive skin, dark hair, and dark eyes. Again, I think, nothing remarkable stands out about him.

I nod instead of taking his hand. I've been bleeding too, and I don't want my blood to mix with his.

"This is Oliver from the Northern Ireland territory," he continues the introductions. "Callum from the Scotland territory and Rhys from Ireland. We owe you..."

"The only thing I want," I interrupt, "is for this to stop here. Were the drugs something you *all* agreed upon?"

"No, ma'am," Rhys replies. His red hair falls into his eyes as he shakes his head.

Callum bravely steps forward, holding his arm close to his body, trying to stop the flow of blood. "Malcolm told us it was the best way to control the people we needed to defeat the Priestess." He bows his head. "I never wanted my people to be addicted and dependent on Malcolm."

I study his bowed, strawberry-blonde head, determining whether to believe them or not.

"Fine. The drugs stop, this foolish revolution ends, and the Enforcers disappear. Do any of you have a problem with those terms?"

They all shake their heads timidly. So, Malcolm was the one who made these guys feel more confident. His grand ideas gave them a false sense of bravado.

"Good. I need you to tell your people to stand down." My tone is so matter-of-fact that it leaves no room for discussion. Even so, they all look at each other with doubt.

"What about Malcolm's? I don't know if they'll listen to us," Roan states. "We can handle our own, but what will become of his followers?"

"They have no one left to follow. At least, not Malcolm. They face a choice: stay with the Society or leave it entirely. But *Malcolm's* way of doing things no longer exists. Now, there's only one way—The Society's way. No one will be forced to do anything they don't want to anymore, but the Society will not tolerate anyone who puts innocents in danger any longer."

"Who will rule this territory?" Miguel asks hesitantly.

"No more Rulers. We have Leaders in the Society—Leaders who respect their Hunters, who treat them like the family they're supposed to be, and who guide them to do the honorable thing. You will meet the Leader of this territory soon. Then, if you're deemed qualified, you'll have the opportunity to lead your own territory. *Only* if you're qualified—and the standards are much higher than just standing behind Malcolm's ideology. Do you understand?" I wait for their agreement before turning to Sam. "Let's get out of here. These guys need to make an announcement."

"What about them?" Sam motions to Malcolm and Gunner.

"Let Roan and the others take them out. Once the declarations are made, we'll give them a proper burial, and their followers will know, for sure, that Malcolm's regime is over. Amanda?"

"Yeah?"

"Come back. Leave Abby's people to handle what's going on. This isn't our problem anymore."

"On our way."

Roan and the others announced to their respective groups to stand down, spreading the word that the Priestess is dead. Moving Malcolm's body out of the house effectively told his followers that he had been defeated, much like the Priestess. They, along with Abby, informed groups from all territories that things will return to the ways of the Society, with some small changes.

True to my word, I ensured Malcolm received a proper burial. However, I refused to give him a Hunters send-off. Too many innocents were hurt or killed because of him to grant that formality. One thing that worries me is that the Cursed Ones Malcolm promised humans to have disappeared. That's not good. If they're not evolved Cursed Ones like Liam, we could face another epidemic. We don't need more Cursed Ones being created by those who aim to use humans as a food source.

However, as I told Amanda, this is no longer our problem. That may seem harsh, but having done this one too many times in my six hundred plus years, I'm done. It is time for me to step back and let someone else take over. Am I sure I can do that completely, especially if my Hunters decide to stay inside? No. But it never hurts to keep an eye on my family and my parents' legacy, right? Even if it is from afar.

CHAPTER TWENTY-SEVEN

Hunters are born to maintain peace between the Cursed Ones and innocents. They are revered for their protection and loyal above all else. They are bound by the rules of the Society. The rules are few, but they are strong. First, your fundamental duty is to protect innocents at all costs - even if it means your own death. Second, you *must* kill any Cursed Ones who are a threat to innocents. If the Cursed One has demonstrated that he/she has retained their humanity and can live peacefully among humans, they can be granted amnesty. If a Cursed One does not abide by the rules of the Society, you must make sure they are dead by either beheading them or setting them on fire. Third, killing a human is still prohibited, unless your own life or the life of others is in danger. It is up to you to determine whether the human is innocent or a menace, and even then, your first recourse is to incapacitate. Death is ONLY acceptable if there are no other alternatives. And, finally, rules are always made to be broken because there are always exceptions.

I once lived by the old rules. Until circumstances made me realize that rules are never black and white, and I needed to break all of them. Would I do it all over again? Yes.

There's a part of me that can't wrap my head around the fact that this is over. For the most part, it ended peacefully with only minimal casualties. It just so happens that those casualties were the "bad guys." To say that I am eternally grateful that all my Hunters are unharmed is a gross understatement. As we now sit around the dining room table—yes, eating again because Jenna was 'starving'—I find myself overwhelmed with emotion.

Baby?

I wink at Sam, giving him a small smile. We just need to wrap up a few details, and then we can go home. Or, honestly, anywhere.

"Abby, have you decided how you're going to handle the other territories?" I ask before taking a bite of my pizza. No, I don't need it, but it sure tastes good.

"We've all decided to meet, sort of like a round table discussion. I don't want to run this place like the Priestess did. I want us to be, well, like all of you." She looks at me and my Hunters. "You rely on each other, and though you're the Leader, Anala, you look to them for help. That's what the Society was before, according to stories I've heard. We want to get that back. I'm happy to say that the other territories are on board with that."

"Sounds like a good plan," I smile. "And, what will you do about the drug problem?"

"First, we get the drugs out of here and get the innocents around here to help. A 'community cleanup', if you will. I'm sure that will be our most difficult task, but with everyone's cooperation, I think we can handle it." She pauses for a moment to take a drink. "We may have trouble with Cursed Ones that expect humans to be their personal blood banks," she says, echoing my own concerns.

"You are Hunters. Cursed Ones do not have free rein to use humans. Those who do not comply with the new rules of the Society are to be eradicated." That, actually, *is* black and white for me. Cursed Ones are not supposed to exist.

Humans are, and will always be, the dominant species. We are, basically, guests in their world. If we break the rules, they have the right to 'kick us out'.

"What will you do?" Abby asks softly.

I shrug and give Sam a grin. "Travel, maybe. I'm not sure. We have an eternity to figure it out." Amanda and the rest of my Hunters remain silent for the rest of the dinner. Sam and I both wonder if it's because they're unhappy with us. That's something we'll all need to discuss before any plans can start.

"I wish you would stay. I'm not sure I'm ready for this."

"Abby, I will always be around if you need help. But you have already proven you're ready for this. You stepped up when you needed to. I have no doubts you'll be an excellent Leader." As I sit at the head of the table, I look at each of my Hunters, and Abby and Liam. "This is a room full of Leaders," I announce softly, spreading my arms wide to encompass them all. "Whether you choose to lead a chapter of the Society or choose a different path in life, you will continue to be someone people can look up to. I am honored to know each and every one of you, and I know that *I* am a better person - a better Leader - because of you." I focus on Amanda, Jenna, Emily, Eric, Jeremy, and Sara. "When I was forced to choose a group of Hunters, descendants from those in my past, I had no idea what I would be getting. I couldn't be more impressed - or more blessed - with what I *did* get. If I *have* to fight for humanity, I would want you all to be by my side. Every time."

Amanda quietly wipes away a tear from her eye, giving me a small smile. We still haven't talked about future plans, but I know, as I hope she does, that she will always be part of my life.

"Who knew you were such a sap?" Jenna, being Jenna, smirks at me, but I notice tears glistening in her eyes as well.

"Who knew you were such a bitch...oh wait, never mind." I wink wryly at the blonde cheerleader, and get the laugh I was hoping for from everyone.

Much later, after Abby and Liam leave, my Hunters and I sit in the makeshift meditation room. We are seated in a circle around a thick lavender-scented candle. The mood is somber, as the group of friends finally realize that this is the moment when we go our separate ways. Whether that means college for the others, I'm not sure. But whatever they choose to do, I will support them both financially and emotionally.

"Have you all thought about what you want to do now?" I ask at length.

They all look at each other, waiting for someone to speak first. No one speaks right away, and then I hear Eric clear his throat.

"I think I want to stay here for a while. Perhaps help Abby out, at least until she gets settled. The rogue Cursed Ones could prove to be troublesome, and I'd like to be able to assist."

I wonder if Eric is purposefully leaving out that he's interested in the new Leader, or if he just hasn't figured it all out yet.

"That sounds like a good idea," I say carefully. "You will be sure to take care of yourself, right? Don't give up on your dreams, Eric."

Eric smiles warmly at me. "I promise. I figure I'll look at colleges around here. I'm actually interested in majoring in political science, perhaps at the University of Oxford."

I chuckle. Told you! He would be a perfect politician. The 'people's politician'. "Good for you, Eric." I glance at Emily, wondering if she would stay here, too.

I think I will stay too, "Emily says quietly, as if she's reading my mind." "I don't know about college yet, but I want to help Abby clean up around here. Plus, I'd like to explore the area a little—see where you grew up," she finishes shyly.

"I'd love to show you around. Maybe we could spend a few days hanging out with each other. As friends."

Emily's smile brightens, as do the others'. I'm even excited about taking them on a tour of my hometown without anything to worry about.

"What about you, Sara? What will you do?"

She looks pensive for a moment, then grins. "I think I'll go back to California. I want to go back to University to continue my studies. I think that's what *mi abuela* would want."

"Excellent. I'm sure your grandmother would be proud of you," I smile brightly. "Jeremy?"

Jeremy sighs, glancing quickly at Jenna. "I don't know yet," he says glumly.

I narrow my eyes, curious about what was happening between him and Jenna. So, I decide to ask Miss Grumpy McGrumperton about her plans. She looks up sharply, appearing almost angry at my question.

"I don't know."

"Jenna, you're really talented with electronics. Why not pursue something in that field?"

Jenna shrugs. "Maybe."

I let both of them off the hook for now, then turn to Amanda. "What will you do?" I ask softly.

Amanda's eyes fill with unshed tears, and it causes my own composure to falter. "I like what I do now," she says tearfully. "I finally found something that I'm good at."

"Oh, Mandy Bear, you will be great at anything you want to do," I tell her sincerely, taking her hand in mine. "Being a Hunter doesn't have to be your life anymore, but it has given you the tools you need to succeed in all parts of your life."

"I know." She wipes away a tear that rolls down her cheek. "But before you came to me with this unbelievable fairytale of a story, I struggled with what I wanted to do with my life. I had no clue. No interests. Now I do. Not just being a Hunter, but learning about the history and making sure future Hunters know the truth about the Society and the Geils."

A stray tear escapes my blurry eyes, but I don't wipe it away. Amanda has honored me more than I deserve.

"So, you will be the official Historian and journalist of the Society," I say with authority. "I've read what you've written, Amanda. You're extremely talented. Maybe you should consider writing a book about your experience. Fiction, of course." I give her a wink, secretly hoping she does write a book. I don't think she realizes just how talented she is, and I can only hope that being a Hunter has given her the confidence in herself she deserves.

She blushes, but her smile reveals everything I need to know. This *is* something she has considered.

"So, what will you and Sam do?" Jenna asks, giving Amanda a sweet backrub and a reprieve from being the center of attention. "Besides each other, of course."

So close. We were so close to having a deep conversation about our future. Then Jenna pulls a Jenna. And, yet, I can't be mad because that's really all I want to do with Sam for at least the first century. Sam lets out a sly snicker, and once again, I'm really glad I can't blush.

"Oh Lord, you guys have nothing planned except that, do you!" Jenna snorts.

"You'll be the first to know what our plans are once we make them, Jenna," Sam promises cheekily.

"That's okay. I don't need details." Jenna shivers exaggeratedly, making crude noises.

"Ahem!" I need to get this conversation back on track before I lose everyone's attention. "I do have something else to say before we make plans for an outing the next few days." I pause to ensure everyone is focused on me again. "I'll try to keep the sappiness down for Jenna's sake, but I wanted to do something for all of you to show how grateful I am that you put your lives on hold - and in danger - for me." I hold my finger up to stop any interruptions. "I have opened trusts for each of you."

They all gasp in what I'm sure is surprise, and start talking over each other. Even Sam is looking at me with amazement.

"You all deserve it," I shout over everyone, and their chatter dies down. "It's a trust that will accumulate over time, as long as you don't spend it in one shopping spree. Jenna." Jenna stares at me, her mouth hanging open. "In addition to that trust, if you decide college is what's right for you, your tuition will be paid in full."

"Ana, that's too much," Amanda declares.

"Hey, let the woman pay if she wants!" Jenna counters jokingly, but I still see the bewilderment in her eyes.

"It's not too much, Amanda. In fact, I'm not sure it's enough, but it's a start. When you all took a leap of faith with me, you *knew* you could very well die doing it. Even when we lost a friend, you never turned your back on me." I see Emily lower her eyes. "Not even you, Emily. Grief is a part of all of this, but you still stuck around. You all followed me, led me, fought with me, forgave me, and believed in me when I didn't believe in myself. You gave me something to live an eternity for." I look at Sam and grin. "So you see, Amanda, it's not too much."

"Thank you, A." Jeremy's voice is sincere and thick with emotion, which I find unusual coming from the quarterback stud who doesn't show emotion easily.

"Sí, gracias," Sara chimes in. Even though she hasn't been with us that long, she has more than proven her loyalty and worth. The others convey their gratitude, including Jenna, with hugs and complete awe.

"Just be happy in your life. Be as great as I know you all are. And remember, I'm always just a phone call away. If you *ever* need me for anything, I'll be there."

CHAPTER TWENTY-EIGHT

"FOREVER."

"**W**hy didn't you tell me about the trusts?"

Sam and I lie in bed, limbs entwined, with my head resting on his strong shoulder. The hurt in his voice makes me reach up and kiss his lips briefly.

"I wasn't hiding anything from you, baby. I set up the trusts as soon as I realized they were all staying. There's even one in your name."

"I don't need..."

"I know, my love. But it's there and it's yours to do whatever you want with."

"Transfer it in Amanda's name."

I lift myself up again and balance on my elbow so I can look into his eyes.

"Okay. Are you worried about her?"

"I'll always be worried about her. She's my baby sister. But I need to trust her to take care of herself."

I smile at him, give him another kiss, and then settle back on his shoulder. My fingers softly trace figure eights on his chest.

"What would you like to do, Sam? We have an eternity to fill up. Do you have anything on your bucket list that you'd like to check off?"

His voice lowers an octave and turns seductive. "Mmmhmm. I can think of a few things."

I can't stop the silly grin. "You know, contrary to what Jenna thinks, we can't just make love all the time."

"Why not? We don't need sleep, we can feed off each other, and I know for a fact that your stamina is unrivaled."

His chest rumbles with laughter when I playfully slap it with mock chagrin.

"I suppose you're right. We should just bunker down somewhere and never see the light of day again. We are vampires, after all. It's what's expected," I tease.

"See? Now you're talkin'. However," Sam rolls away from me, but with his arm tucked underneath me, I roll with him. I assume he's looking for paper or something to actually write down his bucket list of things to do. After a moment of knocking things around on the nightstand, he rolls back into our original position. "There is one thing I would like to do before we 'bunker down.'"

"Oh yeah? What's the one..." My words fade as he places a black velvet box in front of my face. I freeze. I don't look up at him or turn away from the box, or maybe even breathe.

The moment I opened the door that night you came to my parents' house, I saw my forever," Sam murmurs. "It scared me so much to feel that for someone so young in my eyes, so I lashed out. I tried, Anala, to stay away from you, but the pull was just too strong. I needed you as much as I needed to breathe. I wanted you more than I had ever wanted anything or anyone in my life. And now, I know that forever with you is real, and I still fear it's not long enough." He pulls me up until I'm forced to look him in the eye. "There are many labels I can put on you. Lover, Leader, Maker, friend, vampire," he smiles. "But there is one title I long to call you. Wife. Will you marry me, Anala?"

The tears flow freely down my face, and Sam brushes them away with his thumb. Never, in all my centuries, did I believe this would be possible for me. Of course, I could have changed anyone to be my companion forever, but there was never anyone I could see wanting to be around for that long. Until I met Sam and fell so deeply in love that I thought I might die from it. He is the one I want. Forever.

"*Yes.*"

"Yes?"

I claim his lips in a deep, soulful, breath-taking kiss. When I finally pull back, we're both breathing heavily.

"Yes."

His lopsided grin turns into a brilliant smile as he picks up the velvet box and opens it. Inside sits an incredible ring with a stunning, round brilliant two-carat diamond surrounded by a halo of rubies in an octagonal design. Four sparkling side diamonds rest on the platinum band, completing the beautiful piece of jewelry.

"It's gorgeous, Sam."

"You're gorgeous, Anala. This ring will only highlight your beauty."

"My, my. You certainly know how to woo a woman, Detective."

Sam chuckles. "I only want to woo you. And it's not detective anymore. It's fiancé." He takes the ring out of its resting place and slips it onto my finger, then brings both to his lips for a sweet kiss. "I love you, Anala."

"I love you, too."

We took the time to thoroughly celebrate our engagement, making sure we each knew just how happy we were. After a couple of hours, we settle back into our original position, with my head reclining on his shoulder.

"Sam?"

"Yes, baby?"

"Did you really just propose to me, in bed, while we are naked?"

Sam let out a loud belly laugh, and the sound thrills me. What a beautiful, amazing sound it is.

"Yes, I did. But I planned it that way."

"You did?"

"Mmhmm. It saved us a lot of time."

I look up at him again with a wicked grin. "Pretty sure of yourself, aren't ya, stud?"

He shrugs. "It was either you said yes and we make love or you said no, in which case I would have had to persuade you to change your mind." He kisses me lightly on the tip of my nose. "Either way, we were already undressed for the occasion."

"How would you have persuaded me?"

"Doesn't matter, you said yes," he says smugly.

"I take it back."

"Can't."

"Pretend," I urge.

Sam growls and rolls over until he's on top of me. "Eternity with you is going to be so much fun," he rumbles before proceeding to 'persuade' me.

EPILOGUE

"It's been a century..."

So, I bet you're curious about what's happened with everyone, right? I thought so. It's been forever, so let me gather my thoughts and make sure I get everything right. Let's start with me and Sam.

The day after Sam proposed to me, we announced it to the group. They, of course, weren't surprised, but they were very happy for us. To celebrate, all of us spent the next few days together exploring my hometown. We decided to visit the spot where my parents died so I could say goodbye properly. Even now, I swear they stood out among the trees and watched me. It felt like a balm to my soul.

I also showed them the spot where I became what I am today. Now, there have been debates lately about what we should call ourselves. We have evolved so much that calling us Cursed no longer seems, well, politically correct. But I digress. Let's get back to what I was saying. It was amazing - and at times sad - exploring my past through the eyes of a human, not a Cursed One or a Hunter. Just me, Anala, and my friends enjoying our time together and the beauty of the country around us. Those two days are days I will remember forever as two of the best days of my very long life.

Sam and I decided not to have a long engagement, but we did agree to give Amanda, Jenna, Emily, and Sara enough time to plan a small wedding. The boys wore distinguished tuxes - Sam looked incredible. The girls wore pretty summer dresses in bright, cheerful colors. I wore a simple white Vera Wang strapless dress. I fell in love with how the dress hugged my curves, and it turns out, Sam did too. He makes me bring it out every ten years or so, just so he can relive the moment he saw me walking down the aisle.

The wedding was held under a tent where my childhood home once stood. I was hesitant to have our wedding there because of the bad memories, but Amanda persuaded me. She told me to focus on the good memories I had there as a child—when my parents and I were happy, playful, and shared unconditional love. It worked. In fact, I was glad Amanda insisted so strongly because that day, I felt my parents' presence more vividly than ever before.

As for Amanda, well . . . she and Liam go on vacations with us every year. You weren't expecting that, were you? The rules of the Society have evolved as much as we have. For the most part, changing humans is still forbidden. But as the new laws stated, every rule has an exception. *If* you find your soul mate, and both parties agree, you may make the change. However, if that change brings about a true Cursed One—one that has lost its humanity—you *must* kill it. No exceptions. It's a harsh rule, and changing someone you're in love with is risky. But true love makes people take risks they never thought they would. Liam and Amanda did, much to Sam's horror and delight. We just thank God that the change was as positive for Amanda as it was for Sam. And I'm glad that I will have my best friend by my side throughout this life. Amanda continues to write the journals for the Society, in addition to being a successful and best-selling author. She and Liam are the Leaders of their own chapter of the Society in Liam's hometown of Exeter. It is now one of the areas Hunters flock to so they can be trained and led by the best.

I know you're *dying* to hear about Jenna. She and Jeremy *did* end up together. They both returned to California, where they attended college—Jenna earned her master's degree in computer science and Jeremy earned his master's degree in business. Together, they built an empire focused on surveillance technology.

Honestly, they specialized in technology that could detect true Cursed Ones worldwide. Don't ask me how, because algorithms aren't my thing. They would visit us often, and as they grew older, we would visit them. Their funerals, one year apart, with Jenna passing first, were hard. Our only comfort was that they lived long, happy lives into their nineties. Their empire was passed down through generations—yes, Jenna and Jeremy had children—and each generation knows Sam and me, as well as Amanda and Liam, as aunts and uncles. We still watch the family grow and change.

Eric stayed with Abby after he finally realized he was in love and helped her restore the Society. However, his political career took priority, and he left to pursue his future in the States. His charisma and ability to keep his promises made him a popular candidate. He used his position as a U.S. Senator to help bring about much-needed positive changes. Of course, we would visit from wherever we were in the world at the moment. As he aged, he would tell me that his one regret was letting Abby go. He never found another love after that, instead focusing on the greater good rather than his own happiness. He died not long after learning that Abby had been killed in a car accident. He was sixty-three.

Emily traveled the world on the trust I set up for her. When she wasn't sightseeing, she spent her time training Hunters in hand-to-hand combat and, of course, swordsmanship. She became known as the best trainer in the land and was soon sought after by every chapter of the Society. There were even more chapters than I ever imagined, so Emily definitely stayed busy. Sam and I would meet up with Emily whenever she traveled through places we happened to be. She would tell us how she and Eric were still close, but since his political career took up most of his time, they rarely saw each other. Emily was with us when Eric passed away, and we knew the moment it happened. She explained to us later that when Eric died of a heart aneurysm, she felt like half of her soul had died as well. Emily withdrew into herself afterward, rarely emerging from her self-imposed seclusion. We received word that Emily passed away at the age of sixty-five. We'll never know what really happened in that remote cabin just a few miles from where my childhood home once stood. All we know is that Emily was found days after her death, lying peacefully in her bed.

Sara became what we call a 'career student.' She had more degrees than I had centuries under my belt. Every time we spoke, she was busy with her studies for yet another PhD. She became a highly respected professor at her alma mater, UCLA, where she proficiently taught Anthropology, History, and Spanish. We rarely got to see her, though Sam, Amanda, Liam, and I always attended her graduations or showed up for her important life milestones. She married a fellow professor, had children, and grandchildren. But she also decided to keep her Hunter heritage—and the fact that people like me exist in the world—a secret. She said she didn't want her children or grandchildren to have to go through the heartache she experienced in just the short time she was with us. I understood completely. Since we never aged, our visits became less frequent over the years, though Sara would send us emails and photos of her family all the time. Sara lived a long, fulfilling life, finally passing away from natural causes at the age of ninety-two.

So, all that remains of our eclectic group of Hunters are Sam, Amanda, and me. Jenna and Jeremy's descendants, of course, will always be honorary members of the Society, and if any of them ever choose to pursue this path, I would be honored to train them. But for now, we're happy to watch them grow into their own extraordinary lives.

Although we are always on the move, Sam and I have a permanent home on the land where my parents took their last breath. Being there always makes me feel close to them, and we make a point to visit as often as possible.

I'm also happy to report that after a century together, Sam and I remain as in love - if not more so - than we were when we first fell for each other. We have no trouble finding things to keep us busy, and I must say, being a vampire can be wonderful. When you don't need sleep and your stamina is endless, being married to someone like Sam is quite the adventure.

The first six hundred years of my life as a Cursed One were just that—cursed. Now, I find myself anxious for the next six hundred. The one word that comes to mind when I think of the years ahead with Sam? Blessed.

I may have been born destined to kill. But I have no doubt that Sam and I were destined to meet and destined to love each other. Forever.

The End

ACKNOWLEDGMENTS

End credit song: Rescue Me (How the Story Ends) by Kerrie Roberts

As with the last book, we'll get to the original acknowledgements here in a second. If I failed to thank Aven for "forcing" me to re-edit this trilogy for the sake of "readability" for her to narrate, I apologize. You see, these manuscripts were so old that they were formatted completely different than what we do now. Basically, they were a mess. And while I was "cleaning" them up for Aven, I decided to read through them and clean up any tense errors I found. Which were A LOT. I've grown a lot as a writer in the past decade (I hope). I learn from mistakes (or try). Hopefully, by cleaning up Anala's story, I've made it a little better. I had forgotten what a good story this is. Can I say that about my own stories? I do miss Anala, and I hope to continue her story in some way in the future. If my dreams are any indication, I think that's a very real possibility. Now, onto the original acknowledgments:

Well, here it is—the final book in the Destined series. There were times I didn't think this moment would actually arrive. Honestly, I never thought I'd write a young adult novel, let alone one about vampires. But never say never. Anala's story came to me in a dream, which is usually how my books begin. I have a dream, an abstract idea, and then I sit down to write. They don't always turn out as I imagined, but I believe they turn out the way they are meant to. I won't share how I initially thought this story would develop, because I don't think that's fair to myself or to anyone reading this series. I want to avoid 'what ifs.' That said, I will say that there MAY be a novella about Anala and Sam's romantic relationship. Never say never.

Again, I have to thank my beta readers, Daisy, Wanda, Lisa, and Lee - without you all, I would have unnecessary chapters and sentences that don't make sense. You taking the time to read and discuss with me means the world. I rely on people like you to tell me if the story is truly worth telling.

As always, I'm grateful for the support of my family—blood and chosen. Even though my mom knows I will give her as many copies of my books as she wants, she insists on buying her own. Now that's loyalty!

I could never forget the book nerds everywhere. It's a very vulnerable thing for a writer to finish a book and put it out there for anyone to read. I think we all realize that we'll never be able to please everyone. But we can always hope that people will enjoy what you've spent hours, weeks, and months writing. I truly hope you enjoy how I ended this series.

Jim McLaurin (Pops - RIP), proofreader extraordinaire! Thank you for proofreading my last two books! Not only am I impressed with your resume ;) but also with how personable you are! I'm still coming to you with my other books... I hope you don't blush easily! I absolutely adore you!! (RIP)

As always, to my readers - your continued support humbles me. My imagination has always been a bit 'out there.' I've often used it as a coping mechanism when life didn't go my way. I'm grateful I've been able to use it well and hope I've created good books that entertain you. Anala's story has come to a close with this book, which makes me a little sad, but also proud that I saw it through to the end. I truly hope you're as happy with the ending as I am.

My characters are special to me, especially Anala. She's a strong woman with a touch of vulnerability, and I can't help but keep a part of my heart reserved for her. Still, more characters are on the way, and I'm eager to see how they turn out! I truly hope that what I write will touch you in some way.

ABOUT THE AUTHOR

I've called Houston, Texas home since 2009, where I've been writing novels and building the life I love. The arts have always been part of who I am: music sets the mood, reading sparks my mind, and writing lets me explore the limitless corners of my imagination. I've been writing and imagining stories since I was a teen, but I knew it was truly my passion the moment I finished my first novel, *Something About Eve*.

Books have always captivated me, carrying me into exotic worlds and impossible scenarios where I could live as someone else, if only for a while. That same magic drives me to bring my own characters to life. My greatest hope is that my stories inspire readers—or at the very least, give them a welcome escape from everyday life.

Beyond writing, I founded **Jaded Angels LLC**, a business inspired by my beloved momma. Through Jaded Angels, I merge creativity and heart, offering products and stories that honor her memory. Since her passing from Alzheimer's, I've dedicated a portion of my proceeds to supporting those impacted by this devastating disease. Mourning someone who is still alive takes a toll on the soul and losing them entirely shatters it. Writing has been my anchor through grief, and I carry her memory with me in every word. #endalz

Find out more at:

www.jourdynkelly.com

Follow me on social media:

Instagram: @JourdynK
TikTok: @jourdynkelly
Facebook
(https://www.facebook.com/AuthorJourdynKelly)
Secret Society on Facebook
(https://www.facebook.com/groups/JoKels/)

What you should know:

Anala Geil (Ana Gale)

- Daughter of the Leaders of the Society of Hunters.

- Hunter

- Vampire

- Leader of the New Society of Hunters

- The Cloaked One

- Done with high school forever

- Thomas's true Maker

- ·Over 600 years old

- In love with Sam

- Sam's Maker

- Married to Sam

Sam Logan

- Homicide Detective (Retired)

- Amanda's brother

- Hunter

- Descendant of Thomas Lagan

- In love with Anala

- Turned by Anala (to save his life)

- Married to Anala

Amanda Logan

- Ana's best friend

- Sam's sister

- Descendant of Thomas Lagan

- Keeper of the journals

- Best Selling Author

- Hunter

- Turned by Liam

- Eternal connection with Liam

Jenna Hynes

- Ana's biggest champion (surprisingly)

- Hunter

- Mean girl with attitude (but softy on the inside)

- Loves to pop her gum

- Closet geek

- Marries Jeremy

- Builds an empire that is passed down generations

Emily Zhou

- Tried to kill Anala once

- Hunter

- Eric's twin sister

- Fencing expert

- Acrobatic

- Can communicate with Eric via thoughts

- The most sought-after trainer in the Society

Eric Zhou

- U.S. Senator

- Hunter

- Emily's twin brother

- Fencing expert

- Can communicate with Emily via thoughts

- Fell for Abby

- Held regrets until his dying day

Jeremy Trent

- Excelled in business

- Hunter

- Marries Jenna

- Builds empire with Jenna to pass down for generations

Zac Connor

- Hybrid

- Senior in high school

- Turned by Thomas

- In love with Ana

- Crushing on Emily

- Deceased

Thomas Lagan

- Cursed

- Was once a Hunter

- Lost his humanity

- Once loved Anala

- Wants Anala to join him

- Created armies of Hybrids

- Deceased

Innocents

- Humans

Hybrids

- Vampires

- Cursed

- Recently turned

- Cannot turn others

- Not as strong as Full Bloods

Full Bloods

- Vampires

- Cursed

- Hybrids that have completed the change

- Can turn humans

Cursed Ones

- Vampires

- No humanity (with a few exceptions)

- Can turn humans

Elders

- Cursed Ones that have survived the Enforcers and Priestess

- Centuries old

Blood Orchlips

- Man-made flowers created for medicinal purposes

- Ingredient used for Humanity serum

Enforcers

- Group started by Malcolm

- Do not agree that women should be in charge

- Feuding with the Priestess

Liam Culver

- Elder

- Cursed One

- Helps Anala and her Hunters

- Falls for Amanda

Priestess

- Anala Lagan

- 'New' Cloaked One

- Rules with an iron fist

- Believes only women should be in charge

Anala Lagan

- Priestess

- ·Descendant of Emma Lagan

- Arrogant Ruler

Emma Lagan

- Thomas's sister

- Created the "Priestess"

- Wants her descendants to emulate Anala

- Wants complete control of Hunters and innocents

- Cursed One

- Obsessed with Anala

Abby

- Reluctant follower of the Priestess

- Friend of Tania's and Monica's

- Has seniority under the Priestess

- Takes over leading the Society

Tania

- Follower of the Priestess

- Malcolm's sister

- Wants Sam

- Anala's nemesis

- "Frienemy" of Monica's and Abby's

Monica

- Reluctant follower of the Priestess
- Friend of Tania's and Abby's

Roan

- Head of the Netherlands territory
- Reluctant supporter of the Enforcers

Oliver

- Head of Northern Ireland territory
- Reluctant supporter of the Enforcers

Callum

- Head of Scotland territory
- Reluctant supporter of the Enforcers

Rhys

- Head of Ireland territory
- Reluctant supporter of the Enforcers

Miguel

- Head of Spain territory

- Reluctant supporter of the Enforcers